Mysterious Journey

By Alec Price

Fᴀʙᴜʟᴏᴜs BᴏᴏᴋS

www.fbs-publishing.co.uk

Published in the UK February 2015 by FBS Publishing Limited.
22 Dereham Road, Thetford,
Norfolk. IP25 6ER

ISBN 978-0-9560537-9-4

A CIP catalogue record for this book is available from the British
Library.

Text Edited by Alasdair McKenzie
Cover Design by Owen Claxton
Typesetting by Scott Burditt

Paper stock used is natural, recyclable and made from wood grown in
sustainable forests.
The manufacturing processes conform to environmental regulations.

Dedication

All Trogglybog lovers, everywhere.

Long live the Trogglybog Preservation Society.

Mysterious Journey
Contents

Chapter 1

Leaving Pendle

The stable door opened slowly, letting in the cold early morning air. Standing in the doorway was the tall robust figure of the innkeeper. Holding his lamp high, he peered down at the woman wrapped in a blanket and lying huddled on the straw. He was an unkindly sort, whose mistrust of the woman became obvious in the tone of his voice.

'Here, a bowl of porridge. As soon as you've finished that, be on your way, and remember—not a word to anyone that I gave you shelter this night,' said the man.

The woman stared up at the dark silhouette of the innkeeper. She thanked him, and as she took the steaming bowl from him she gave her word that she would tell no one. He nodded his head then turned, closing the door behind him. The stable had been a welcome retreat from the cold and wet of the day before. The heat from the animals' bodies had created a cosy warmth, though the smell was a little off-putting at times, even for a country woman such as she was.

A few moments later, the innkeeper's wife entered the dark stable. She passed the woman a parcel of bread and some cheese wrapped in muslin cloth.

'Take this … You'll need something for your journey, and be sure to wrap up well; there's a bad day ahead.'

Even though she was afraid of the woman, the wife was only too aware of the hardship facing the poor wretch that day, and the weather was set to be just as unkind as the people she would meet as she went on her way.

It was mid-November in the year of our Lord 1602. The woman in question was Alice Bond, well known and equally feared around these parts. Many suspected her of being a witch. It was rumoured that certain things had happened to people who had been unfortunate enough to have had—shall we say—'disagreements' with her. Things that some of them hadn't lived to tell of. Others who had survived such encounters had ended up with brain illness or disfigurements.

Nothing could ever be proved, and the only thing the woman had ever been whipped for was for not attending chapel on Sundays. The local magistrate was well aware of the rumours, but was unable to act without evidence. Alice was now well into her fifties, a stout woman who had developed a strong will thanks to the way folks had treated her. She had lived in the Pendle area for most of her life, save for a period of one year when she had moved to Devon to care for a sickly aunt.

It was said that her mother had despaired of her and couldn't cope with Alice in her teens. Sending her to her aunt's was a temporary relief, but after she returned she was a changed person. She appeared to be more of a woman than a teenage girl. It wasn't long after her return that her mother died suddenly, but nothing untoward was suspected at the time.

Alice had her mother buried in the churchyard

at Whalley. She was given a full Christian burial. As the years passed, Alice distanced herself from the rest of her family, and most of her neighbours. She became known for having sympathies with other members of the community who had been suspected of strange misdoings, and was often seen leaving Malkin Tower at the top of Pendle Brook. She had also been heard laughing and screeching out loud with old Demdike and the simpleton they called Chatox. These were not the kind of people that good, decent folk associated with, and this added more weight to suspicions that all was not right with Alice Bond.

Residing alone in her late mother's tiny cottage in the hamlet of Sabden, the only company she kept was her cat, a few hens and a goat. She earned a half-decent living as a seamstress. She did have relatives in Whalley, but she only ever saw them when she attended Whalley church on Sundays, and, even then, none of them had much to say to her, nor she to them.

It was their view that Alice had no place in God's house, that she was indeed a godless person. They had no proof that she had ever been involved in wrongdoing, but they had all heard the rumours and stood by the belief that there is no smoke where there is no fire.

On the morning of Friday the 13th of November, Alice Bond received a visit from one Anne Redfern, another undesirable. Why Redfern wanted Alice was not for telling, but whatever it was, it had the woman in a state of some excitement.

As her visitor left, Alice paid a call on her

neighbour Daniel Wilcocks and requested that he look after her hens and goat, saying that she had to go away for a few days. She didn't say on what business, and Daniel didn't ask. He was a quiet, unassuming man who kept himself to himself, looking after his small holding and working for a local farmer, tending the sheep. He kindly agreed to look after the animals for as long as was needed.

Alice quickly sought out some warm travelling clothes and her sturdy walking shoes. The journey she was going on would take her over the moors, south west towards the market town of Chorley. It would not be the easiest of journeys and would take her a good four days before she reached her destination. Why she had been instructed to go that way is unknown. It meant she would have to walk over the top of Pendle, across to Haslingden, over the Grane Moor and on to Darwen Moor, Withnell and Brinscall Moors; a difficult journey for anyone, least of all a woman at the onset of winter.

The following morning, when all arrangements had been made and her animals settled, she secured her house and set off. It was hardly daylight when she took to the road over Pendle Hill. Instead of heading towards Read, Alice went to Barley. There she met with a woman by the name of Elizabeth Preston, who gave her a parcel to take with her. She was to deliver it to a gentleman of some standing, by the name of Cedric Hoghton of Chorley.

All Alice knew of the parcel was that it contained two stones that, when placed together with three others of a kind, would unlock secrets of great powers beyond belief. She was told to be wary of certain people on her travels. There were those who would go to any lengths to have these stones. She was to tell no-one the purpose of her journey or her destination.

After spending no more than a few minutes with Mistress Preston, Alice was on her way again, this time heading towards Haslingden Moor. The weather on that first morning wasn't too bad—overcast but dry. The only company she had over the hill were some sheep that grazed and wandered freely.

Within the hour, she had made good progress and was soon on the lower reaches at the far side of Pendle Hill and heading towards Gawthorpe Hall, not that she would be calling there. She had no liking for the folk of Gawthorpe, and she knew that they would hold similar sentiments for her. She took a wide berth around the hall and carried on towards Padiham, a small settlement just north-west of the township of Burnley. She had friends at Padiham and she decided she would call on them for some refreshment.

She had gone no more than half a mile past Gawthorpe when she was almost mown down by three horsemen galloping like the wind towards Pendle. The first she knew of their coming was the thundering sound of hooves, and then from round a hedgerow they were upon her. She hardly had a chance to move out of the way.

Startled by the speed of the horses, she glowered at the three men. She immediately recognised one of the horsemen as Richard Darnley. He was the magistrate's right-hand man. He stopped only for a second, then when he saw it was Alice Bond he didn't bother to ask if she was all right. He turned again, and without a word he was off in the direction of his friends. The look on his face spoke volumes for what folk around these parts thought of Alice. Uninjured, she brushed herself down and scowled at the man as he rode away.

Just after lunchtime, Alice arrived at the house where her friend lived. She was welcomed and fed, which was just as well; it just might be the only meal she would get that day. She knew no one over Haslingden way, but it was quite probable that Alice would have been heard of in those parts. News tended to travel freely. People like Alice Bond were openly discussed and avoided whenever possible. Before leaving, Alice collected some wild herbs that grew around the friend's cottage. She placed them in a bag, along with some she had picked on her way. Then she bid her friend good day and set off again.

She made good time that first day, and it was just getting dark when she arrived at the old coaching house on the Haslingden road. She was about to approach the front of the inn when the innkeeper's wife saw her and called to her not to go inside. Beckoning her to the rear of the stables, she asked her what her business was. Alice replied that all she wanted was somewhere to sleep for the night. The coach house appeared to be deserted. No travellers had called there for a room that day.

It was then that the innkeeper came out into the yard and saw Alice and his wife together. Straightaway he knew who she was and told her to be on her way. Alice pleaded with him not to turn her away, saying she meant him no harm—all she wanted was somewhere to sleep for the night. The innkeeper's wife asked what harm it would do to give the woman shelter for the night. After a moment, the man relented.

'Very well, you can sleep in the stable, but no one must know you're here or that you've been here and I want you gone before first light. Understood?'

Alice agreed, and gave her word that she would be no trouble. The wife showed Alice to the stable. She scattered a deep bed of fresh straw and gave her a blanket. Alice settled down, and after a while the innkeeper's wife came in to see her again, this time with a bowl of hot broth. This was unusual, as Alice Bond wasn't used to such kindness, and it took her by surprise. Once she had finished her meal, she settled down. The long day had taken its toll. The warmth from the animals in the stables helped her to relax, and she was soon fast asleep.

Her first day had soon passed and the night had been untroubled. After finishing her bowl of porridge, she placed the bread and cheese in her shoulder bag along with the parcel from Mistress Preston and the herbs and berries she'd collected the previous day.

She was soon aware of what the innkeeper's wife had meant by there being a bad day ahead. As she opened the stable door and walked into the yard, the bitter wind hit her. She quickly pulled her shawl tighter around her shoulders and looked up towards the sky. It was still dark, but with no sign of any stars, which told her there were plenty of clouds;

and that could mean rain.

'It's not the best of days. Do you have far to go?' asked the innkeeper's wife. Alice looked at her. "Far enough" was the reply as she walked out of the yard.

Turning right in the direction of Darwen, Alice stumbled her way along the rough path that was full of broken stones; this was a poor excuse for a cart track and was ankle breaking ground for anyone. The further she walked, the more she tripped and almost fell. She soon realised that it would be better to wait for daylight, and sat down on a large rock by the side of the track.

The day ahead would be fraught with danger. Alice knew this, and she also knew that she had to make good time in order to reach the far side of Darwen by nightfall. Beyond the Darwen Moor lay the hamlet of Tockholes and a large wood. Word had it that the wood was haunted by the spirit of a man known only as the Gatekeeper.

He was said to be an evil sort who had been bewitched by demons and eaten alive by troglodytes, or so the story went! His spirit is still said to live on today, and terrorises all who dare to pass through the wood. Mind you, most of these tales had come from those who had left the alehouse at the top of Tockholes Heights, but none had been brave enough or foolish enough to seek the truth of such tales.

She had heard all these stories, but was unafraid. Alice herself was well able to deal with this 'Gatekeeper', thanks to her powers, and in some ways, she was relishing the prospect.

But first she had to pass through Darwen, a

deeply religious township and a place where many a suspected witch had been put to the stake. The advice given to her was to look no one in the eye and to keep walking as she passed through. She was also strongly advised to avoid the Bull Hill, a place of residence for Sir Thomas Henry James, a well known Witchfinder. The prospect of passing through Darwen alarmed Alice more than Tockholes Wood.

The day was slow arriving. The large grey clouds hampered its much needed light, but as soon as there was enough to be able to see the unevenness of the track, Alice decided she could waste no more of the day, and she set off westward towards Darwen. She hadn't travelled more than a hundred yards when she saw a wooden sign that indicated her way.

It was a long brow of a hill, and then a steep path down that led to the hamlet of Hoddlesden. It revealed a small, unwelcoming clutch of huts and smallholdings. Smoke rose from the centre of some of them. The only thing that stirred was a farmer who was going about his business. He looked at Alice and stared suspiciously. It was a rare sight to see a stranger, and especially a woman alone and at such an early time of day.

The man carried on staring, but Alice put her head down and walked on through the row of huts. As she walked on, a dog barked at her, and then another and another, as if they were passing on a warning of a trespasser within their midst. The farmer shouted at the dog to 'Be quiet,' but it took no notice.

The noise brought the women out of their huts and away from their chores. All were keen to see who or what was causing such a racket. Alice didn't look at any of them; she just carried on walking and ignored it all.

Soon she was through the tiny hamlet, and one by one the dogs fell silent as she got more distant. In front of her was another large hill. The track was no more even on this side than it had been on her approach to Hoddlesden. As she started to climb the long path, the rain started. She pulled her cape over shoulders and held it tight to her front.

As she reached the top of the hill, she noticed a man walking parallel to her, about a hundred yards to her left but going in the same direction. Something told her he was up to mischief. He had his head down, but every so often he looked up and in her direction. The man was in quite a rush to get to wherever he was going. Alice suspected she might have cause for concern.

On reaching the highest point of the hill, the man was ahead of Alice and was definitely heading in the direction of Darwen. She could see the township ahead of her. It could be no more than a mile away. Alice stopped, and took stock of how she was going to set her journey around this 'witch-hating' place, and from where she was standing and from what her friends had told her she suspected Bull Hill was far to her left.

She could see a large house on the top of a hill. It had smoke coming from its large stack. It was obvious even from such a distance that this was the residence of someone of high standing, and very likely it was Sir Thomas Henry James' house.

The man who had been walking in her direction was indeed heading towards that house. He was walking at quite a pace. Occasionally, he would turn and look in Alice's direction. It was clear to her that this man's mission was to alert Sir Thomas to her presence. It amazed her how people knew who she was, when she hadn't ever been through their part of the world before. What didn't amaze her was the hatred she could sense from the looks she had been given as she made her way over these inhospitable hills.

It was now mid-morning, and Alice Bond knew she had little time to stand and stare at the scenery. Quickening her pace, she set off downhill in the direction of the town. After a while, she arrived at a fork in the road. One path led towards the centre of the town—this was also the direction of Bull Hill, and Sir Thomas's house.

The other path took her northwards, away from the town. Alice now had the dilemma of whether or not to risk going into the town itself, or heading away from it and making her journey much longer by a further five miles. Time was against her. It was approaching midday, and if Alice was to reach the far side of the town and the moor beyond before nightfall, she could not afford a further five miles' walking. She decided to take her chances, and took the left path towards the centre of the town.

Chapter 2

Sir Thomas Henry James–Witchfinder

Walking down from the hilltop into Darwen didn't take as long as she thought it might, and the town itself appeared to be nothing out of the ordinary. It was Saturday and the town's market was in full flow. Local farmers were busy touting their wares and the weavers were showing their cloth to all who wished to look. The local folk seemed to be enjoying the hustle and bustle of the day and took no notice of the stranger within their midst.

With only one objective in mind, Alice made her way through the crowds of traders and buyers, keeping herself to herself and making eye contact with no one. The market square was surrounded by stone cottages and wooden houses, with almost as many shops and alehouses as there were private residences. It was a clean, neat little township that appeared to have a charm of its own.

Halfway through the square against a wall was a drinking trough with an iron stand pump. Alice made her way towards it to fill her water canteen. Horses were standing around and some of the men were sitting by their horses, drinking their ale and laughing amongst themselves. None of them so much as glanced at Alice as she proceeded to fill her canteen.

Suddenly, there was a commotion in the centre of the square. Hens flew everywhere, men shouted and women screamed. Four horsemen rode into the centre of the square; they were flanked by six others on foot. All were carrying pikestaffs. The lead horseman drew his sword, held it high above his head and began to address the crowds.

Alice knew this was trouble. She quickly took her water canteen and placed it back in her shoulder bag. All the men who had been sitting around talking were now on their feet and looking in the direction of the commotion, but none of them took any notice of Alice.

She quickly and quietly slipped behind the horses and through a small gap in the wall. Once behind the wall, she looked around for the safest way out of the square. The voice of the man who was addressing the crowd was, without any doubt, that of Sir Thomas Henry James, the Witchfinder.

'Hear me all of you. There is a woman in our midst that is evil and dangerous. She is here on murderous business and none of you are safe while she is at liberty. All of you must go from here now and search your homes and your farmsteads. Look in your outbuildings and your byres. Word has reached me from the Pendle district that his woman has committed deeds of unmentionable cruelty to those who have helped her ... Some have even perished at her hand. Waste no time— bring her to me and I will deliver her to justice.'

The large crowd shouted and whooped in support. Soon the whole town would be looking for Alice Bond, and she knew it. In front of her was the backyard of a blacksmith's place. Alice ran across, and entered the open door. The owner had obviously gone into the square to see what all the fuss was about. Once inside, she saw a ladder leading up to the loft.

Alice quickly climbed the ladder and made her way to the far end of the loft, where there was straw stored. She got as far to the back as she could and hid against the wall, pulling the straw on top of her. She couldn't have been there more than a few minutes when she heard voices—men were downstairs and searching the place. Then footsteps made the boards of the loft bounce and creak. She knew someone was there, but she made no movement and hardly drew breath in a bid not to draw attention to herself. She could hear the man moving about, and the sound of him poking something into the pile of straw near her made her close her eyes with fear.

A pitchfork passed within inches of her. It was so close that it went through her cape and the shoulder bag she was carrying, but luckily it missed her body.

'There's no one up here,' shouted the man. Alice, much to her relief, heard him climb down the ladder. All went quiet and then she heard the ladder being climbed again. This time there was more than one pair of footsteps coming into the loft. Quickly, and without any warning, two men were in amongst the pile of straw and were soon dragging Alice out. One of them held a dagger to her neck.

'Well, what have we here? She doesn't look all that evil, but we'll take her to Sir Thomas anyway— we might just get a reward.' The men almost threw Alice down out of the loft. Their treatment of her caused Alice to swear revenge upon them.

Alice noticed water dripping from the ceiling of the loft and assumed that the pitchfork that had come so close to stabbing her must have pierced her water bottle. The men had seen the water dripping from the ceiling, and knowing they didn't store water in the loft, they realised there must be someone up there.

In all the commotion Alice had left her bag in the loft, and along with it the stones from Mistress Preston. All she could do was hope that noeone would find the bag.

The man dragged Alice out of the blacksmith's workshop and through the street to the square, where Sir Thomas was having a flagon of ale while his men did the searching. He quickly stood up as the three men came along, dragging Alice with them. She stumbled a few times, falling and dirtying herself in the filth of the square, where the animals had been fouling. By the time she reached Sir Thomas, she was a mess. Sir Thomas asked her name, where she was from and what her business was in the town.

Alice thought fast, and spoke with a Devon accent. It had been something she had picked up during her time living down there with her aunt.

'My name is Agnes Downes and I'm from Brixham in Devon. I'm just passing through on my way to visit relatives in Chorley.'

Alice's accent was very good and had Sir Thomas asking her to repeat what she had said because he couldn't understand her. Then he asked what business she had in the loft of the blacksmiths. She told him she had travelled a long way the day before and was weary. She said she had slept in there from the middle of the night.

Sir Thomas asked how she had got in if the

building was locked. She said it wasn't locked when she tried the door. She continued.

'Sir, it was raining and pitch-black when I arrived here and needed shelter for the night. I just tried the door and it was open. It was my intention to be gone by first light, but I must have been so tired that I slept through. The straw was so welcoming and comfortable.'

'If you are travelling as you say, woman, where are your belongings?' asked Sir Thomas.

'I was accosted about ten miles from here at a place known as the Pendle area. A woman with deep black eyes and a pointed face threatened me and took all I had. I knew I hadn't far to go and was hoping for some charity along my journey to sustain my needs. I never meant to trespass or to cause anyone any concern, sir.' Alice bowed her head apologetically.

Sir Thomas said nothing for a moment. He just looked at Alice and then whispered to the man on his right. The man came over and looked closely at Alice, lifting her cape and searching her person. He turned to Sir Thomas and shook his head. Sir Thomas then called forward the man whom Alice had seen walking near to her along the moor from Hoddlesden. Sir Thomas thanked the man for his observations, and then he struck him across the face with his glove and told him to be sure of his facts in future rather than waste his valuable time.

'This is clearly not the woman we have been warned of. Set the wretch free.' With that he finished his drink and mounted his horse. Alice's broad Devon accent had worked. How thankful for it she was. Sir Thomas rode off and everyone went about their business. The market in the square was by this time coming to a close and people and farmers were packing their wares ready for the journey home.

Alice's concern was for her bag and its contents, but there was no chance of her returning to the blacksmith's shed now. There would be too much suspicion of her motives. She decided to make her way to the edge of the town and return after dark. This had delayed Alice's plans by at least half a day, maybe longer.

Alice had to walk only a few hundred yards and she was free of the town. She crossed a coach track and climbed a stile on to the edge of the moor. She saw a shepherd's hut just at the foot of the hill. It was open and empty, so she went inside and waited for darkness to fall. It was cold and damp inside. There was some wood and other kindling, but she didn't want to draw any attention to herself, so she just huddled up in the corner to keep warm.

Darkness came, but Alice decided to wait until she was sure everyone was settled down for the night. She waited for what must have felt like a lifetime with no company but for the odd sheep calling outside and an owl screeching as it hunted in the darkness. It had been dark for hours by now, and Alice could stand the wait no longer. She crept out of the hut and looked down from the hill towards the sleeping township of Darwen. She could not see any lights, just the glowing embers of an odd fire or two burning.

She made her way down to the stile, and once over, she crossed the track and was soon back in the streets of the town again. She followed the street that led to the town's square. Alice found the water trough and the gap in the wall where she had gone through to the blacksmith's.

The door to the blacksmith's was unlocked, and she entered slowly. The door creaked as she opened it, and a dog barked at hearing the noise. Alice waited and looked around to see if any lights were lit, but none were; thankfully, the dog stopped barking.

Alice fumbled her way around and found the ladder still leaning against the loft. She slowly and quietly climbed the ladder to the loft. Once on top she walked across towards the pile of straw where she had been. The boards creaked with every step she took.

She bent down and began to look for her bag. She searched everywhere, from one end of the loft to the other, but her bag wasn't there. Suddenly, the whole place lit up, as six men bearing torches entered the building. With them was Sir Thomas Henry James.

'Looking for this, are you, woman?' he asked, holding up her sackcloth bag.

He gave her the option. 'Come down here now, or I'll send my men up there to throw you down.' He was in no mood for reasoning.

Alice climbed down the ladder, and when she was a few rungs from the bottom she was grabbed by two of the men and manhandled out of the shed. The party took her back to the centre of the square, but as she was being dragged through the doors of the blacksmith's workshop she noticed the forge was still glowing. She smiled to herself and muttered something.

'Save your mutterings for the court, woman,' said one of the guards, who were holding her arms.

Behind them in the blacksmith's shop, the bellows had begun to lift and fall slowly all by themselves, and then they started to rise and fall faster and faster. The forge was soon glowing hot, hotter than it ever had before.

Sir Thomas had instructed the innkeeper to open the inn; it was decided to hold court there that night. Within ten minutes, the inn was full of men from the town. All were ordering ale and laughing at Alice as she stood in a makeshift dock made out of upturned tables.

Sir Thomas sat at the top end of the room with his two henchmen at either side of him. Two others stood by Alice. Also, there was the man who had followed Alice across the moor earlier that morning. This time, however, it was obvious he was in Sir Thomas's favour.

Sir Thomas called the room to order, banging on the table with his riding crop. He raised his head and looked Alice squarely in the eye.

'So, woman, you lied? You told us you had no belongings, you said you had been accosted and robbed, yet here we find a bag with herbs and berries and a parcel with two odd-looking runes inside it.' He held up the bag and tipped its contents onto the table in front of him. Out fell the stones that were of such importance to Alice. They were the whole purpose of her journey.

'These may be the tools of witchcraft. Some may say that a woman of such great powers could work any manner of mischief with items such as these. What do you have to say, woman? Don't give me that excuse of being a traveller from Devon. I do not believe a word of it.'

Before Alice could answer, a shout went up.

'Come, quickly, the blacksmith's shop is on fire.' Everyone except Alice and the two guards holding her ran outside to see what was happening. The fire was taking hold, and men were running about with buckets to and fro from the horse trough.

Alice smiled to herself and muttered something else. The guards looked at her and knew this was possibly her doing. Then a wind blew up and the fire raged even more, with flames reaching high into the night sky and wafting all around. Sparks from the fire were blowing everywhere, and very soon other houses and shops were taking hold too.

The entire town was now out on the streets and frantically fighting the fire that was threatening all their homes. Panic was setting in. The roof of the inn had now caught fire and the two guards didn't know what to do. Alice laughed, and looked at the two men.

'You'll save yourselves, if you've any sense,' she said, and then she laughed more and louder still.

The two men left Alice and ran outside, leaving her to collect her bag and its very precious contents and to flee amidst the pandemonium. Alice made her way back to the stile and fled across the fields away from Darwen Township. She knew she had to get as far away as she could, and quickly.

She was in no doubt that Sir Thomas would hunt her down as soon as the fire was dowsed. He was, for the time being, too preoccupied with trying to save the town; but she knew he would muster every man available and lay chase at daybreak, to hunt her down like some wild animal.

Alice made haste across the fields towards Darwen Hill, and although the land she was rushing over was rough and sodden with all the rain that had fallen in the past few days, it was nothing to what she would have to struggle over when she reached the hill and the boggy moorland that lay beyond.

Luck was on Alice's side; there was no moon that night, and even though it made it hard for her to see her way over the fields, it meant she could not be seen by anyone who might be looking for her. After an hour of stumbling her way across the barren fields, she finally reached the foot of the huge hill that overlooked Darwen.

The climb in front of her was something that resembled Pendle Hill. It was high and its sides were steep. Water washed down gullies, and the sodden ground was very slippery. Alice managed to find a sheep run that weaved and wound its way up the hillside, and although water was running down it like a small stream the ground was fairly solid.

Alice began the long climb up the hill, and at times she found the going so hard that she had to claw her way up on her hands and knees. It wasn't long before she was wet through. The weight of her wet clothes made the climb even harder. Her feet were wet and her boots were rubbing her feet so badly that the blisters she already had were now bleeding and extremely painful, but there was no time to stop to dress her wounds.

Time was against her, and she realised that the men of the town would be able to cope with the hill and the elements far better than she could. It took Alice the best part of the entire night to reach the top of Darwen Hill, and even when she did reach the top, she still had a long way to go before she had any hope of safety from Sir Thomas's men.

Alice had been climbing for about two hours when she reached a shepherd's hut. She turned around for the first time and looked back towards the town. There were still flames glowing in the night sky. She had no idea of the time or how long it would be before daybreak, but her feet were in such a state that she thought it would be an advantage to dry them and bind them. The pain she was enduring was unbearable. She couldn't go on any further without doing something.

Alice wasted no time; she tore her petticoat into strips and bound her feet. Her petticoat was the only dry clothing she had; she was shivering with the cold. In the darkness of the shepherd's hut, Alice fumbled around and found some sacking cloth. She took off her cloak and wrapped the sacking around her; putting her wet cloak over the top.

She wasted no more time and set off further up the hill. There seemed to be no end to the side of this huge outcrop. On both sides of the sheep track, the terrain was rough, covered in bracken and heather and rocks. The darkness hampered Alice just as much as the rushing water. It was ankle-breaking ground, and it would have been difficult enough in daylight, let alone pitch darkness but, surprisingly, Alice's eyesight had become accustomed to the dark.

Some hours later, Alice finally reached the top of the hill, and for the second time she turned to look back towards the township of Darwen. There was no glow coming from the town now. The fire must have been put out. She knew that was bad, because it meant Sir Thomas was now free to pursue her. She wasn't wrong. As she looked down the hillside, she could see rows of torches spread out for about a mile across the fields below.

The sound of dogs barking accompanied the line of torches. Alice knew she had to make haste. Her best hope was to find her way to Tockholes Wood as quickly as she could. For all the fearsome tales that she had been told of this place, she felt she would rather take her chances there than with Sir Thomas and his men. Alice Bond had some measures of her own that she hoped would keep her safe from the Gatekeeper and whatever other dark dangers the wood held.

It was difficult terrain for Alice. The light was bad, but would soon improve. She could see the glow of daylight coming over the hilltops in the East. This was both good and bad news for the poor woman. Good that she would be able to see where she was going, but it would also be an advantage to Sir Thomas's men too.

The ground was extremely rough, with large tufts of grass and heather, and unlike Haslingden Moor, Alice could hardly find any sheep runs to follow in the dark. She had no idea if she was even heading in the right direction. All she could do was hope and keep going.

As the day broke over the top of the moor, Alice looked back to see if she could see or hear anything of her pursuers, but there was nothing to give her any indication of where they were or if they were even still following her, but she couldn't take any chances. She had to keep moving as fast and as far away from Darwen as she could.

By this time, Alice was beginning to go downhill, and with the better daylight she could see a huge mass of woodland in the distance. That had to be Tockholes Wood, she thought to herself, but it was a long way off. By now, Alice was very tired and hungry. She took out some of the bread from her bag that the innkeeper's wife had given her. It was more than a full day since she had eaten anything.

He ate, still walking as fast as her weary legs would carry her. Suddenly, and without warning, the ground fell away from her as the hillside almost became a cliff top. She stopped and looked downwards at the steep ravine that lay in front of her, and thanked God that she hadn't reached this in the darkness. If she had, she would have fallen down what must have been more than three hundred feet to the bottom of the ravine. At the bottom she could see a stream gushing its way down to the lower reaches of the moor.

Alice walked further along the hilltop, trying to find a safer way down. She was in luck. There was a sheep track that appeared to wind its way down and sideways. The ground was firm, not slippery. Quickly, but steadily, Alice made her way downwards using her stick to balance herself against the steep sides of the hill. Still listening, she couldn't hear any sounds of dogs or men, but Alice was not foolish enough to imagine that Sir Thomas would have given up.

It took her a good half hour to reach safe ground. Now she had to find a way across what had only appeared as a stream from the top of the hill. Standing close up alongside it, she saw that it was now a raging torrent, and if she attempted to cross it or even fell in, she knew she would be swept to her death by the force of the water.

Alice walked along the path that had continued from the top of the moor. Rounding a bend in the stream, she saw a wooden footbridge, and on the other side a small hut that had smoke coming from a hole in its roof. Alice had no choice; she had to cross the bridge. She took her time, tiptoeing as she went in the hope that she would not draw attention to herself.

She had no way of knowing who might be inside the hut, be it one of Sir Thomas's men or some other undesirable who might take her for the bounty. Once she had walked across the footbridge, the path took her straight past the door of the hut. She held her breath and prayed there was no dog around to alert the inhabitants. No dog barked, indeed there was no sound at all, and Alice was beginning to wonder if there was anyone at home.

Rather than risk being caught, she decided not to take the chance of finding out and she slowly made her way past the hut. Head down and creeping as quietly as she could, she was past the door by a good two yards when she heard it slam behind her. She turned around quickly expecting to see someone, but there was no one there. Turning again, she came face to face with the ugliest, most gnarled man she had ever seen.

He was bent over and only stood at around four feet. His red hair was long and his beard was also red and long, but dirty and full of matted food. His eyes were uneven, which matched his teeth, and his breath stank.

'What are you after here, woman?' he shouted at Alice with his head cocked to the side in an inquisitive pose.

'I'm not after anything, I am simply a traveller passing through. I mean you no harm,' said Alice.

'Mean me no harm ... Mean me no harm.' He laughed out loud. 'I could eat you for my dinner, and no trouble ... Mean me no harm, indeed!' He laughed again. 'No travellers ever pass this way; there isn't no way to pass to, save for the black hole of the wood, and nobody who likes living ever goes in there ... So where are you going?' he asked again.

'That is exactly where I'm going. I have to pass through there to reach my destination. I don't have any choice,' said Alice.

'Then you are walking dead,' he said as he squinted and stared at Alice.

'Why haven't you gone the road way round? It might be longer, but at least you will arrive there with your heart still in your bosom. If you go through there, your heart will end up as a meal for him.'

'And who exactly is "him?' asked Alice.

'Why, the Gatekeeper, of course. Don't tell me you never hear o' him.' said the strange little man.

'I've heard of him, but what is your concern, and who are you? Are you one of Sir Thomas's men?' asked Alice.

The man laughed out loud again and jumped up and down.

'Ah, now I see it—you're wanted by Thomas aren't you? And that's why you're heading to the wood. Well, you'll be safe from him in there, all right; he won't follow you in there, that's for sure.' The man laughed even louder. 'If you are intent on going into hell, you must have a good reason. Not even Thomas's rope can be worse than what is in there. Will you trust me woman?' asked the man.

'I don't even know your name or anything about you. Why should I trust you?' asked Alice.

'As I see it, you don't have much choice. I smelt the smoke from last night, and Thomas's men will be here in a couple of hours. I am no friend of Thomas—I owe him no favours. It is because of him that I am like I am. He sent me into the wood, and that is why I ended up like this.' The man raised his arms so as to show Alice his deformed frame.

'My name is Seth, but now they call me Dregs. I fell afoul of Sir Thomas and had to flee to the wood for safety. Unlike you, I had heard of the Gatekeeper and the evil stories that follow him, but I took the stories lightly. That was a big mistake! After only two hours in the wood he found me and … well, I won't tell you no more; it's too horrible. But when I managed to escape, I came back like this. Sir Thomas doesn't recognise me the way I look now, and that suits me; I am safe from the woodsman and from Sir Thomas … Come!' He waved to Alice to follow him.

Reluctantly, she followed him into his hut, which was small but warm. He went into a corner and pulled out a bag. Reaching into the bag, he pulled out a tiny purse made of sheepskin.

'This is Milo. If it wasn't for Milo, I would never have escaped from the wood alive. Use Milo well and look after him.' The tiny bag moved. Dregs opened up the top and placed the open end onto his hand.

A small fleck of light emerged. It bounced and hovered on his hand and then flew around the hut before stopping and dancing in front of Alice's face. Alice lent backwards, not knowing what was to happen next. She smiled, and Milo danced again before flying back to Dregs' open hand. He placed Milo on his shoulder and reached inside the purse again. This time he pulled out what appeared to be a small ball of mist.

'This is Fog. Fog will also protect you, but even these two little friends of mine cannot guarantee your total safety from the evil powers of the Gatekeeper. He is cunning and cruel. If you are carrying anything of worth, he will not rest until he has possession of it.'

Alice stared at Dregs. Did he know what she was carrying, she wondered? The look in his eye offered a question, a suspicion, but of what? Alice was unsure. She smiled, and assured him that what she had were only her own personal possessions and of no worth to the Gatekeeper or anyone else. His face was serious now. He said nothing, and returned Milo and Fog to the tiny purse before handing it to Alice.

'Milo will be your light and your lookout in the dark wood. Use him well. Fog will hide you in times of fear; there will be many of those before you are free of the wood.' And with that, Dregs laughed loudly and jumped around the room.

'How did you come by these two strange gifts?' enquired Alice.

'There was an old woman who tended the Gatekeeper. She fed him and washed his clothes in return for her keep. She took a chance and helped me to escape. I fear the Gatekeeper may have learned of her treachery. I don't know what became of her after I fled.' Dregs bowed his head, and Alice thought she saw a tear fall, but Alice Bond had little time for sentiment.

'I had better make my move. Sir Thomas's men will be upon me soon,' she announced.

'Fear not, woman; Sir Thomas and his men are not trying to catch you, merely to drive you towards the wood. They know where you're heading, and are relishing your fate.' Dregs laughed again and danced once more.

'You are going to have a hard day; the land you have to cross is wet bogland. Many a traveller has been lost up there on the Darwen Moor. The hill to the top will test you even before you reach the top, and it will be near to darkness before you reach the wood. My advice to you is to wait until morning before entering the wood. There is a disused bothy about five hundred paces from the wood. Take shelter there for the night.' Dregs' look spoke enough to assure Alice that he was seriously trying to help her and that his words were wise words.

Alice made her way to the door and turned to thank Dregs. He just shook his head and waved her away.

'Good luck,' he shouted as she made her way towards the sheep track. It wasn't long before Alice understood what Dregs had meant about the hill being testing. As she began the long climb she could smell the smoke from the fire of the night before, and when she had almost reached the top, she turned and looked across to the other side of the ravine. There, standing on top of the far side, were Sir Thomas and his men. They had stopped and were in the middle of having a meal.

As the crow flies, he wasn't more than a few hundred yards away. She could sense the smile on his face as he waved to her.

'Enjoy your freedom while you can, old woman.' His voice boomed out across the valley. His men cheered and waved their sticks, and the dogs with them barked with excitement.

Alice believed Dregs had been right. Sir Thomas was in no hurry to catch her. He knew there was only one way she could go. The wood was no more than a mile ahead of her across the open bogland of the moor, and no matter which way she went it would lead her to the huge dark wood. There was no turning back.

Once she was here, on the top of the hill, the sheep tracks ended without reason. There were no more safe paths. It was now down to her. Looking at the surface of the moor, it looked just like any other part, covered in tufts of rough grass, and large swathes of purple heather bathed it like a sea. The moor was still. Not one animal of any kind in sight. Hardly surprising if it was as inhospitable as Dregs had said it was.

She turned and looked again across the valley towards Sir Thomas and his men. Five or six of them with dogs had begun to make their way down the steep far side of the hill. She suspected this was just to keep her moving. The rest of them remained where they were and continued with their meal.

Looking skywards, Alice was aware of the rain that was no more than a few hours away. Walking using her trusty staff to test the ground, she made her way forward as quickly and safely as she could. Occasionally, she found the ground to be very soft, and after an hour and about one mile in distance, she was becoming quite expert at where not to tread.

Suddenly, the danger of the terrain became all too apparent as she glanced to her left. Sticking out of the ground was what was left of the forearm of some poor soul who had obviously fallen into a deep bog and had quite clearly perished there. Alice turned away, hoping that she would not become the moor's next victim.

Every so often she would look back to see if there was any sign of Sir Thomas's men and their dogs, but nothing and no one came into sight, much to her relief.

The light was beginning to fail when, in the distance, she saw the outline of the old bothy that Dregs had spoken about. She would soon be there, and she was comfortable in the thought that if Sir Thomas's men were attempting to cross the moor in the dark, they would be in serious trouble.

Alice opened the door to the bothy and was pleased to find some dry kindling and wood inside. At least she would be warm and dry until the morning. She lit a fire and cleared off the bench, which was at best dusty and at worst crawling with bugs, but there was nowhere else to rest.

Alice opened her bag and took out what bits of bread and cheese she had left. Staring at it made her realise that unless she could find more food or catch something to eat, she would be very hungry before she had made her way through the wood.

She sat curled up, and stared at the fire as the flames danced and the logs glowed red. She was warm now and relaxed for the first time in two days. Her thoughts were of the Gatekeeper. She wondered what kind of man he really was and why he was so evil. Alice knew of many forms of evil and had a few tricks of her own, but was her trickery any match for this man?

She also wondered how she had allowed herself to be talked into this situation. She was well aware of the power of the goods she was carrying, but did the Gatekeeper know what she had in her possession, and if so, how had he learned of her precious cargo?

Alice woke up shivering and to the sound of rain falling on the roof of the bothy. It was still dark and the fire was almost out. Alice quickly found a few dry twigs and rekindled the flames. As the fire burst back to life, lighting the room, she noticed a strange bag on the bench next to her. She opened it to find more cheese and bread, and some apples. It was all fresh and the bread was still warm. Where could it have come from? She wondered if Dregs had been and left it there for her whilst she slept.

Her journey was indeed getting stranger by the hour, but she suspected there would be far stranger events ahead of her if what she had been told of the wood were true. She took the food and placed it in her shoulder bag.

As soon as it was light enough Alice stepped out of the bothy into the cold wet morning. Ahead of her was a small hill. She knew the wood must be beyond the top of that hill, and taking no chances she again used her staff to test the firmness of the ground.

In no time at all, Alice Bond was standing on top of the hill, and there in front of her was Tockholes Wood, huge and dark and oozing mystery. It stretched as far as the eye could see in both directions. She turned and looked back across the rain- sodden moor from where she had come. There was no sign of Sir Thomas's men, or anyone else for that matter.

Taking a deep breath, she walked down the hill to the wood. There were no fences or walls or any form of barrier around the outer side of the wood. Alice stopped and looked into the darkness that was to become the next part of her journey. She had no idea what part of the wood the Gatekeeper might be in. She knew she would have to take her chances and hope that it wasn't in any part that she needed to pass through. Nor did she know how far it was to the other side and safety.

Chapter 3

Tockholes Wood

This was it. Alice set off. The wood was densely covered in bracken and brambles, making it quite difficult to pass through in parts. Alice had been told of a stream that flowed down through the wood and out at the bottom side. She hoped she would find this and follow it through.

She listened for the sound of running water but couldn't hear anything. Not so much as a bird was singing. The silence of Tockholes Wood was eerie. Slowly she made her way, trying not to create any noise that would give away her presence to the Gatekeeper.

Occasionally, she would stop to listen for running water or for the sound of any other movement, possibly of persons who may be of the undesirable sort, but nothing was stirring. This half pleased her and half disappointed her. The wood was a vast space of darkness—a darkness of a sinister kind! She could sense the evil and mystery there, but couldn't see or hear anything that gave her cause to worry.

Alice decided to follow a path to the left of the way she had been travelling. Her train of thought was that this may lead to the stream she had been told of. The further she walked, the darker it got. The wood became more and more overgrown. Trees that had fallen over the years covered the paths, and weeds, brambles and other foliage had wrapped themselves around the fallen trunks and branches, making it virtually impossible to pass in places.

Alice tried to find ways around, and where possible, she did climb over. She wondered if there might have been a huge storm at one time with the amount of debris that was around.

After struggling for what could only have been half an hour, Alice was worn out. The constant climbing over tree trunks had taken its toll. She sat for a while on one of the fallen trees to catch her breath. While sitting there, she listened again for the sound of water trickling, but nothing!

Then just as she was about to get up and begin again, she thought she heard something. She listened again and held her breath, trying to hear more clearly. There it was again, far in the distance … The sound of a child crying!

Alice wondered if she was near the end of the wood, possibly close to someone's cottage—or might it be a trick, being played on her by the Gatekeeper? She decided to carry on heading in the same direction she had been going in the hope that it would lead her towards the stream. She even wondered if the crying might have been the sound of the stream being distorted by the wood, with all the trees and obstacles that were around.

As she set off in the direction where she thought the crying was coming from, she walked along a path that was deep in fallen autumn leaves. What was strange was how dry the leaves were, considering the rain that had fallen. This was probably because the wood was so dense and overgrown. More than likely the rain had not reached the floor of the wood, thus keeping it as dry as it was.

Every so often, a shaft of daylight would break through the tall canopy of the trees. This was a welcome sight in such a dark, unwelcoming place. Even with the trees bare of foliage, hardly any light came through. Where it did break through, Alice tried to see if there was any sign of life, but there was nothing.

She had walked for no more than five or ten minutes when she again heard the sound of crying. This time it was much clearer and certainly nearer. Alice found herself walking along a path of broken trees and deep tangled undergrowth. There was no alternative but to carry on. It was almost like a corridor that was leading her somewhere on purpose.

The path twisted and turned and sometimes rose and then fell away. Alice wasn't scared, but she did become suspicious that there was some mischief afoot, and quite probably it had something to do with this Gatekeeper fellow.

After a while, the path ended and Alice came into the middle of a clearing. Huge oak trees, beeches and elms, rose and twisted all around the clearing. Their branches tangled as if embracing one another, but at the same time, blocking out the daylight. On the far side there were three paths leading away in different directions.

This was becoming a game. Alice knew this, but had no idea how to play, and nor did she wish to. Her mission was to reach her destination, and she had not accounted for this game. Standing in the centre of the clearing, Alice could hear the crying more distinctly than ever. It appeared to be coming from one of the pathways, but she couldn't make out which one.

Then she remembered the tiny bag that Dregs had given her. In it was Milo, the small fleck of light. Dregs had told her that Milo would show her the way. Opening the bag, she held out her hand and called for Milo to come out. On to her hand danced the small light. Alice looked at it and spoke.

'Milo, show me the way out of here.' Then she lifted her hand as if releasing a dove into the sky.

The tiny light danced around for a moment and then shot off with incredible speed, heading down the path on the left. After no longer than a minute, Milo returned. Then Alice asked another question.

'Milo, is that the path from where I can hear crying?' The light danced up and down and then again went to the same path before returning and resting on Alice's hand.

Alice had no choice but to trust the light that Dregs had said would keep her safe. She looked around and listened, but could see no sign of life, and all she could hear was the sound of a child in some distress. Placing Milo back into the tiny bag, she headed down the path that had been shown to her.

She had walked no more than a few yards before the left side of the path became a steep rock face, and on the other side to the right, the ground fell away into a deep gorge. It was very dark and the whole place gave her a feeling of apprehension. She could sense the evil in these woods, and although she hadn't met with the Gatekeeper, she knew there was something or someone that would at some point soon make themselves known.

The path took a sharp left hand turn and then stopped suddenly. Fallen trees completely blocked the way in front of her and the steep side of the gorge to her right. Precisely where the path had ended, there was the low entrance to what appeared to be a cave leading into the rocks that towered high above her.

She was faced with a dilemma. Did she go back or did she go into the cave and see if there was a way through? Alice had a feeling that she was being led into a trap. In one way, it scared her. In another way, it provoked her to the point of her wanting to meet this Gatekeeper—or at least the spirit of the man that once was.

Alice took a moment to ponder and then entered the cave. She quickly took Milo out of the bag and instructed the tiny light to show her the way. Milo glowed brightly in the darkness and lit the way.

Once inside, the cave opened up into a large open cavern. Water trickled down the sides and ran along a gully that grew in size the further she went. Soon the small gully was more like a river as more water ran down the walls, feeding it. The water was flowing inwards to the cave rather than away towards the entrance. Alice considered this might be a good sign. The water had to go somewhere and maybe it would lead her to where she wanted to go.

After following Milo for ten minutes or so along the edge of the now fast-flowing stream of water, she was forced to stop as the water fell away downwards into darkness. The path Alice had been following took a sharp turn to the left and then meandered downwards for around a hundred yards. Alice had the feeling she must now be quite deep underground.

On reaching the bottom of the winding path, Alice stopped and called to Milo to come to her. The fleck of light did as was asked of it and landed on Alice's hand.

'I don't know where we are going, my little friend, but I fear this path is leading us further away from where I should be going and quite possibly into some degree of danger. I think we should go back. Lead the way, Milo.' The light lifted off Alice's hand and danced around before moving further into the cave and not the way Alice had asked.

'Milo that is not what I said. We must make our way back, this way.' Alice pointed towards the path she had come from, but the light was having none of it and continued to dance and move towards the path that led further into the cave. Without the light that Milo provided, Alice would not be able to find her way back in the darkness. She was now becoming quite afraid, but she had been told by Dregs that Milo would keep her safe. Alice Bond had no choice but to trust this strange little light.

'Oh, very well!' she said out loud. She began to follow Milo down the path. As she made her way, the sound of the child crying was there again and it was getting louder with each yard. Ahead of her, Alice could see light glowing in the darkness. A few minutes later she entered a large open cavern with a huge lagoon. Running down the side was water which she assumed must have been the stream that she had followed earlier.

Alice could hear the sound of the child so very clearly now and knew it must be near. All around the side of the lagoon there were torches fixed to the walls, lighting the whole cavern. The water was inky black and still. The side of the lagoon was littered with rocks and large old dead tree trunks. Alice wondered how such huge tree trunks could have ended up so deep underground and how long they had been there.

She walked around the side of the lagoon, and there, in between the rocks and one of the large fallen tree trunks, there was a child, lying on a bed of straw and wrapped in a blanket. As soon as Alice bent down, the child stopped crying. It looked at her and smiled. Alice had no knowledge of children or their ways, but she estimated this child must have been about one year old. She had no clue at that point as to its being a boy or a girl, and she certainly had no intention of finding out without good cause.

All sorts of thoughts and questions raced through Alice's mind. How had the child got there? Who did it belong to? Was there anyone with the child? Did it need food? What, indeed, did a child of that age eat? Questions flooded her mind, but there were no answers to the questions. What on earth should she do? She couldn't leave it there.

She looked around and then called out to see if there was anyone around. Surely the child couldn't be alone so deep underground? Alice called out again, but no one came.

'Hello, is there anyone here?' Again there was no reply.

All the time the child looked at her pleadingly. Eventually, Alice bent down to pick the child up, but as her hands reached out to it, the child changed, its face taking on a fearsome look. Its smile turned to a growl, showing large wolf-like fangs. Its mouth began to froth, and then the child adopted an all-fours position before jumping on top of a rock. Alice stepped back sharply as fear gripped her for a moment. Then, she regained herself and she looked at the creature and stared at it.

After a few seconds it lowered its gaze, turned and crept away. Alice watched the creature as it left the cavern, going down a tunnel some yards away. Seconds later, a loud growl came from the tunnel. Alice reached inside her muslin bag and fumbled inside the tiny purse that Dregs had given her. She took out the small ball of mist that Dregs referred to as 'Fog'. Alice held it, and looking straight at it, instructed Fog to do its job. Immediately, the small ball engulfed her and she was hidden.

Out of the tunnel came another loud roar, but instead of some wild animal, a man emerged. Again the roar came from the tunnel behind him. He turned and shouted at whatever was making the noise to be quiet. The creature fell silent.

The man was a tall, thin sort, dressed in black and wearing a black felt hat. He had a full beard that matched the colour of his cloth. He looked in the direction of Alice as she stood perfectly still, hoping Fog was successful in its purpose.

Slowly, he bowed his head and shook it, and then he laughed out loud, the sound echoing around the chamber of the huge cavern with deafening effect. He raised his head again, looking in Alice's direction. Alice remained still.

'Oh dear woman, how naïve of you, and I thought you were clever and wary and worthy of much more, but my little friend Dregs really did take you in. I must commend him.'

The fog that had engulfed Alice disappeared as fast as it had appeared, leaving her exposed and in full view.

'There, that's much better, don't you think?' said the man.

Any fear that Alice had left her, and a feeling of anger took its place. She scowled at the man and muttered to herself before pointing straight at him.

'Are you the one they call the Gatekeeper?'

He looked at her, tilting his head. He smiled, scratched his beard and then doffed his hat, bowing slightly.

'I am he, madam, at your service,' he said. Then, replacing his hat, he laughed once more before stopping suddenly and staring at Alice with a look that left her in no doubt that he was in charge of this situation. For a moment there was a deafening silence. Then he spoke.

'I know your reason for coming this way and I know of your precious cargo. I had Dregs guide you here. You thought he was helping you … how wrong! Although he did save you from the flames of Sir Thomas's pyre, did he not? You see, Sir Thomas would have no knowledge of the strange runes you carry or their importance, but when word reached me from Pendle, I knew I would have to protect you from the clutches of Thomas the Witchfinder. It was

Dregs who started the fire in the town that gave you the chance to save your own skin, and it was dear Dregs that guided you to me. He laid the paths out in the wood. His story of woe obviously convinced you to trust him.' His eyes widened.

'The whole purpose of all this is for you to give me those stones that you carry. You obviously have no idea of their significance or the power they hold, but I do. They will unlock the spell that imprisons me and keeps me in this dark and miserable wood.'

'You are supposed to take them to a man called Cedric Hoghton, who thinks once he has the stones he will have the power to unlock many secrets. He thinks he knows where the other three stones are. What he doesn't know is that I also know where those stones are. Once all five runes are placed together, the person who connects them will have powers like no other man … I intend to be that person.'

Alice knew she was in a perilous situation, and also realised that this man was evil as well as being determined. She was also quite mindful of what he may be capable of if he had possession of such power. She had been warned before leaving that she must tell no one of her journey or the cargo she was carrying. She knew full well the importance of her getting these stones to Cedric Hoghton at Chorley.

How did this Gatekeeper know all this? She had no way of escape, and decided instead to try to talk her way out of the predicament.

'If I do give you the stones, what of me?' she asked.

'Dear lady, you are free to go, but it is not a matter

of if you give the stones; I will take those stones. All that is to be decided by you is whether I take them from you by force, or you do the sensible thing and hand them to me.' The Gatekeeper looked at her and held out his hand.

Alice laughed. 'I haven't come all this way to give you anything, and why do you consider it was I who was chosen to deliver these stones? It wasn't because I knew the way over these hills. It was because I have powers of my own that are unequalled by any others.' Alice lifted her head defiantly. Her behaviour surprised the man, and for a moment Alice thought she had caused him to have some doubts. He turned away from her and clapped his hands.

Out of the darkness of the cave came Dregs. His face twisted and his body bent over, he appeared in some pain. He walked over to the Gatekeeper and bowed his head as he acknowledged him. The tall figure of the Gatekeeper touched Dregs by laying his hand on his head. Dregs took a sharp, deep breath and fell to his knees, then after a moment or two he lifted his head and stood up.

The man that stood was not the disfigured Dregs that had just been on his knees. This man was huge, as big as an Ox. He stood up straight and stretched, making his form even larger. Alice stepped back. She was shocked, but didn't allow herself to show any signs of fear.

'So, woman, you have powers. Let me see these powers you speak of. Can they equal this? And will they protect you from Dregs, or Seth as he is now?' The Gatekeeper smiled with a newfound confidence. As he did, Seth stamped his foot hard, causing the whole ground to shake.

Alice bent down and picked up two stones from the ground. She held them in her hand and stretched out her arm, then quickly drew it back and rubbed the stones together in her hands, turning them to sand in seconds.

'Take one step towards me and it will be the last you see of the stones that you find so important.'

Seth moved forward by one step only, before the Gatekeeper stopped him. Then, waving his hand, he shooed Seth away and off back to the darkness of the cavern.

'Very impressive! Let's talk a while.' He held out his arm, inviting her towards the passage where Seth had gone. 'Don't worry, Seth will not harm you or make any attempt to take the stones from you. You have my word.' Alice looked at him and for some reason she believed him. She walked in the direction he had indicated, keeping the stones close to her.

The Gatekeeper walked on for no more than five minutes with Alice close by until they emerged from the cave and into a clearing in the wood. In the clearing was a rather impressive wooden house, quite large, with two floors. To the side of the house was a pen with some pigs and hens and another pen with some goats.

At the front of the house there was a raised wooden porch. A horse was tethered to a tree and was eating grass that had obviously been cut earlier that day. All this took Alice by surprise, that such civilisation should be in a dark hidden place like this. From behind the house came the noise of someone chopping wood. Alice assumed that this must have been Seth at work, but then she heard the sound of a woman laughing and a child playing.

Alice was by now totally confused by all this. How could the spirit of a man with such a reputation of murderous power live like a normal man with people and belongings that were most common in towns and large villages? This man they called the Gatekeeper was an imposing figure, standing well over six feet, but of quite a lean build. His dress was that of a woodsman, albeit a woodsman of some authority. His manner was certainly aloof.

He walked to the door of his house, opening it. He invited Alice inside. Reluctantly, she walked in. The inside was also that of a man of some standing, with fine furnishings. There was a fire burning in the hearth, and Alice welcomed the warmth. Offering her some refreshment, which she accepted, he suggested they might have a lot in common and thought it a good idea to try to reach an amicable solution to the predicament they found themselves in. His manner had changed. He said he would tell Alice all about himself and then allow her to make up her own mind about the reputation that preceded him.

Offering her a chair, he poured her a drink from a cask of ale that rested on a dresser. Alice took the tankard from him and sniffed the contents. The Gatekeeper laughed, and then drank first.

'Don't worry, dear lady. I am not of a mind to try to drug you. I think we can sort our differences in a friendlier manner.' He raised his own tankard, and bowing his head, took a drink.

'You must be wondering how I came to be here in this wood, and where I acquired such a hatred of people, or should I say, how others developed such a hatred of me?'

'I'm listening,' said Alice.'

'There is magic and misdoings involved in my life, but I am the victim, as you will learn if you will, pray, give me the chance to explain.'

'I was no more than a woodsman here for many years, until one day a man came riding through these parts. He said his mission was to find the runes of Merlin that had been left here when the great wizard had stayed in these hills many centuries before. At that time, I knew nothing of the stones that he spoke of. The man went on to tell me of Merlin and the legend of the stones.

'Merlin is said to have rested here when Arthur rode north to raise an army. The old wizard was well cared for by the folks that farmed around here, and it is said that he made magic of a piece of stone before smashing it into five pieces. The five pieces were sent far and wide, but with a promise that if ever the people of these hills needed help, the five stones would reappear and be brought together, thus giving the person reuniting them great powers. It is said the stones can only create goodness …'

Alice raised her hand. 'If they can only do what is good, what did a man with such a reputation for evil want them for, and, for that same reason, what does a man of your character hope to gain from possessing them.'

'As I was about to say … the man who came by

was indeed a man of great evil. I hadn't heard of these stones before that day, but made a joke to him that if I had them, I would ask them to change him from his evil ways. He took great offence at what I said, and cursed me. That man was a Moor, who had come across from the Arab lands with Richard. He had ridden with Richard the Lionheart in the Crusades—that was in the year 1360, but I learned that he was from a time long before that. He had travelled through time for centuries.

He had great magic and he cursed me to stay in these woods and live here forever. I have come to mistrust and despise all those who roam freely. My hatred consumes me and makes me do things I know to be wrong, but I cannot help myself. I must have those stones, and then I can free myself of this curse.' The Gatekeeper's head dropped and he stared at the floor for some time.

'Are you trying to tell me that you have been here since the fourteenth century?' asked Alice.

'It is true. I was a good man, a woodsman with a family until he came. Not anymore. Every so often, the evil that the Moor cursed me with surfaces, and this is usually when I feel threatened. It takes a lot from me to retain my composure, but if I lose that composure-heaven help anyone who is in my way. I am trying to stay calm here, but I need those stones and I will do anything to lay my hands on them.' The man shook his head as if he was fighting within himself. He turned from Alice and was muttering. Then he turned back. His eyes had turned blood red and his face grimaced in pain.

'I do not wish to harm you, but the anger is

building inside me. I am trying to suppress it, but I cannot hold it forever.' By now, the Gatekeeper was beginning to shake. His head was jolting violently from side to side.

Alice shouted at him, telling him she didn't have the stones with her but knew where they were. She told him that she had hidden them as a precaution before entering the wood. She suggested he let her go and she would bring the stones to him. She promised him this was the truth.

He hunched himself into a ball and stayed there, curled up in his world of pain and anger, breathing deeply. Eventually, he lifted his head and told Alice he would let her go for the stones, but he would send Seth with her to be sure of no trickery. Alice agreed.

The Gatekeeper called Seth, and told him to make ready to go with Alice and not to let her out of his sight. Seth nodded, and rushed off to collect some provisions for the trip. He had no idea where they would be going or how long it would take. He suspected it would be no more than a day's trip, because that would take them back as far as the township of Darwen, and he knew Alice had the stones when she was there last.

Although he hadn't seen them when she was at his hut, he suspected she would not have left them behind where Sir Thomas could have laid his hands upon them.

Alice was devious, and although Seth was a big man with great strength, she felt that she was a match for him with her wit and her cunning, but she did not show these feelings. She needed the opportunity to be away from the Gatekeeper and to get out of Tockholes Wood. She looked at the Gatekeeper and bowed her head in acknowledgement to him.

She had no idea if what he had told her was the truth or whether or not it was a ploy to take the stones from her, but she also knew what her own mission was, and was determined to see it through. They set off.

Seth led the way up a winding narrow path that was covered with dense undergrowth. They passed a steep rocky outcrop and were soon out into the opening in the wood. After walking for a while, Seth stopped. He looked around and seemed distracted.

'What's the matter?' asked Alice. 'Why have we stopped?'

Seth knelt down and put his ear to the ground. 'Horses, lots of horses, are coming this way. About a mile away now … must hide!' Seth got up, and grabbing Alice's hand he turned back towards where they had come. Then he stopped again suddenly.

'What now?' asked Alice. Seth looked one way and then the other. He looked scared and confused.

'It's changed; it's not there.'

'What's not there? You're not making any sense.'

Still holding her hand, he set off running deep into the wood. He kept saying it had changed, it had changed.

Then he looked at her and said—'Not again. 'Please not again.' Alice had no idea what Seth meant, but she could tell by the fear in his face that something was seriously wrong, but what it was she had no idea.

'Where are we going? What are you afraid of?'

They were running so fast that they fell over, tumbling down an embankment into a steep ravine that had a stream flowing through the bottom. Uninjured, they scrambled to the side.

'Closer—they're almost here,' he said. Suddenly, Alice could hear the sound of the hooves thudding hard and fast against the ground. Seth dragged her close to the banking of the stream and put his hand over her mouth. The roots of the trees above stuck out of the banking and provided cover. They turned to face the muddy bank and kept deathly still. Soon, the noise of the horses and their snorting told them that they were right above them. The beasts stopped, and one of the riders spoke. It wasn't a voice that had a local sound to it, and Alice struggled to understand what was being said.

'Behold, a beck from which we can take refreshment. Further down we will rest and make camp for the night. It makes no haste to advance this day.'

They rode off slowly. Seth took Alice's hand and quietly made off in the opposite direction to the riders. When they came to a place where the bank was low enough to climb, Seth carefully made his way up and held out his hand for Alice. Once on top, he took her away in the opposite direction from where the horsemen had gone. After a while, they stopped where the wood was dense.

'Right! Are you going to tell me what is going on? Those were not Sir Thomas's men, but you knew that, so who were they?'

Seth looked at Alice and shook his head. 'This has happened to me before. We are in great danger and I don't know how to get us back,' he said. Alice asked what he meant.

'We have gone back to the time of Arthur, one thousand years back, and those men are looking for him. This has happened before. They are bad, evil men who will kill anyone who gets in their way.'

'I fear you are down with the fever, or the Gatekeeper has given you a potion,' said Alice.

'You heard their voices. You saw them, the way they were dressed. Did they look or sound like any men from this time?' asked Seth. 'What I tell you is the truth. Once before, many years ago, after I had left the Gatekeeper's lair, I found myself back in the time from where the stranger from the Arab lands had come. He cursed my master, and by some strange occurrence he had taken me back. I was still in the wood, but a different wood. Believe me, Sir Thomas James is a pup compared to these men.'

'These men are at war with Arthur and are looking for him. At the time when I was last in this place, Arthur was travelling these hills, raising an army to fight Morgana. I fear we have gone back to that time again. The Moor is the man you heard speaking in the strange voice. He is looking for Arthur. He is Bordagan, a general of Morgana. He will stop at nothing and will kill anyone who stands in his way. It is said that he has powers to rival the wizard Merlin. If that is true, Arthur is not safe, and neither are we.'

Seth led the way through the maze of trees and undergrowth, along a rocky path and out into a clearing, but he didn't recognise any of it. The wood was different, far darker, and the foliage was denser.

After walking for what seemed like half a day, there was at last a glimpse of sunlight. The wood ended and there was open space in front of him and the bewildered Alice. Seth thought they had come out on the Darwen side of the moor, but it was difficult to tell—not that it mattered, because the moor had changed, and of course there was no Darwen in this unforgiving time in which they had now arrived. One blessing was that they had no need to fear coming up against Sir Thomas. But now Bordagan was the torment, and he was far more dangerous than Sir Thomas James.

Alice suggested trying to go back into the wood and finding the Gatekeeper's house. Seth laughed. 'You foolish woman! We are a thousand years back in time. There is no Gatekeeper!'

'Then what are we going to do, and where will we go?' asked Alice, her main concern being how they could get back to her own time so that she could fulfil the task she had set out to do.

'I have no idea yet, but we need to make our way to the far side of the wood. There will be people living there on that side of the moors, and I do believe that is where the wizard Merlin will be. It is our only hope. We must avoid Bordagan and his cut-throats at all costs. It will be safer if we stay inside the wood, but close to the edge. That way, we won't get lost; we will have cover, but we will also see any undesirables who come towards the wood.'

Alice had no option but to trust Seth. By now she was cold, and the late afternoon air was beginning to starve her bones. Seth suggested it was impossible to light a fire. It would attract too much attention. He said they must keep walking until the light would no longer allow them to. The path they followed led them down a steep embankment and round a rocky crag. Luck was on their side. They came to an opening that looked like the entrance to a cavern. Seth stopped. He whispered to Alice to be quiet.

'Remember we are in a time long before ours. This could be the lair of some wild beast.' He bent down and picked up a large stone. He threw it as hard as he could into the cavern. It clattered and bounced, but nothing stirred.

'Come, I think we are safe in here.' He picked up some dry grass and wrapped it around a stick, making a torch, and then he lit it and made his way inside the cavern. It was dry, and after a few feet the passage took a bend to the right. Seth said he thought it would be safe enough to make a fire and shelter there for the night.

This was indeed welcome news to Alice's ears. By now she was very cold, and she was shivering. Seth gathered some wood and made a fire in the corner of the cavern. After having some food, Alice listened as he told her all about his last experience of getting lost in time in Tockholes Wood—how it happened without warning and how suddenly he was back in his own time again without any form of explanation or reason.

'These woods are bewitched. So many unexplained things happen here. I am sure Bordagan is the root of the evil that lives here. He has a hold on these woods that is timeless,' he said.

'If this is true, then why do we not leave the woods and make our way by another path?' asked

Alice. She knew this was dangerous, but what could be as bad as the evil of Tockholes Wood?

Seth shook his head. 'If we break cover and Bordagan's scouts see us, we are finished. We are better staying close to the edge of the wood and following it all the way around until we reach the other side.'

'And what then? Will we be in the open country once we reach the other side?'

'Yes, but we will at least be in countryside that is occupied by people. That is, providing Bordagan and his men haven't slaughtered everyone. So sleep now. We have a long day ahead tomorrow.'

Alice was weary. It felt as if every day was longer and more troubled than the last one. She pulled her cape tight over her head and closed her eyes. As she lay there, she tried to make sense of what was happening. She could not understand how she had suddenly been taken back in time. To her, one wood was pretty much like any other, and yet Seth was convinced this had happened to him before. It was all too confusing for Alice. She was soon asleep.

Seth, however, couldn't sleep. He lay there wondering why these things kept happening to him. How did he come to be back again in the time of Bordagan and Arthur? What was the purpose of it all? So many questions raced through his head. And what of Alice Bond? This woman who had fallen foul of the mystery and mayhem, what part did she play in all this? At first he thought it must have something to do with the stones, but then he realised the stones didn't even exist yet in this time that he now found himself in. Merlin would only have created them later.

Alice Bond had been unfortunate to be caught up in some strange time warp, and Seth had no idea how to get the pair of them back to his own time. The last time this had happened was equally as odd as their current predicament, and he had no idea how he had got back the last time. He knew he would just have to take his chances and try to avoid Bordagan and his men.

If he and Alice could find their way to the Brinscall Moor, where it was said Merlin was in hiding, they might find a way of unravelling this mystery, but the Brinscall Moor was more than day's walk away, and the open country they had to cross would leave them very exposed. First, they had to find their way around Tockholes Wood. Seth had no knowledge of the size of the wood, only that it spread for miles in every direction.

This was now the sixth century, and much would have changed from then to the time he was from. As the night wore on, Seth did eventually fall asleep. The warmth from the fire relaxed him, and the soft sound of the crackling of the logs as they burned calmed his troubled thoughts.

Chapter 4

Fleeing From the Moor

Alice and Seth woke with a start to the sound of howling. The fire had died right down and was almost out. Seth quickly put more dry grass and wood on to the dying embers, bringing it back to life. Alice asked what the howling was.

'Wolves, no doubt,' replied Seth.

'There are still wolves around here?' asked a surprised Alice. She had again forgotten that she was now in a time when wolves still roamed the countryside.

Alice Bond lived in what was known as Lancashire, but the time she now found herself in, there was no such place as 'Lancashire.' This was a part of Northumbria—south-western Northumbria, to be precise. It was a place and a time when wolves, and even bears, roamed freely. And if legend had its place, there were far more fearsome creatures to be worried about.

Seth told Alice to stay close by the fire. He would go and see how near the wolf pack was. He had been gone quite some time. Alice was getting worried, and was just about to go and look for him when he returned, carrying with him two large staffs that he had carved from young sapling trees. He had sharpened points at one end.

'These should offer some protection, if we need it,' he said, passing one to Alice.

Alice was clearly bewildered by all that was

happening to her. She wondered if her own brand of spells and wizardry would be any use at all in this strange place.

'What of the two pieces of protection you gave me—Fog and Milo? Do they not offer any protection here?' asked Alice.

Seth looked at her and shrugged his shoulders. 'I don't know, have you still got them?'

Alice rummaged through the bag and found the small pouch that Seth had given to her. She passed it to Seth. He held it upside down and shook the bag. Out fell the small ball of mist and then followed Milo, a tiny flicker of light. Seth smiled and so did Alice.

Then he picked them up and held them in the palm of his hand. 'We may need your help, my two little friends.'

Seth kicked dirt over the fire, putting it out, and then told Alice it was time to leave. They stepped outside the cavern, and could see daylight just about breaking through the treetops. Leading the way, Seth headed uphill towards where he thought the edge of the wood would be nearest.

They had gone no more than few yards when a piercing howl from a wolf came from just behind them. Seth turned quickly, his sharpened staff at the ready, but there was no animal to be seen. Again, the howl echoed through the wood. It sounded more to the left. Then it came again, this time from the right. Grabbing Alice by the hand, Seth set off and ran, dragging the poor woman almost off her feet.

The howling stopped, and then a loud burst of piercing laughter replaced it. One man was making the sound, but it was a laugh of evil measure. Seth carried on running with Alice. They reached a bank of earth and hid behind it. Seth fumbled for the small ball of mist that was Fog and shook it all around and over them both.

Fear filled the pair of them as the evil laughter became louder and much nearer. Then it stopped as suddenly as it began. Seth looked at Alice and indicated to her not to make a sound. He had no idea if they were alone or if whatever was making the noise was still there with them. They stayed as still as the ground for what seemed like an age.

When Seth finally decided to break free from the mist that had become their sanctuary, he looked around, but could not see or hear anyone. He waved his hand and gathered Fog back into the tiny ball of mist again, placing it back in the pouch.

Slowly, he and Alice got up from behind the muddy bank and set off upwards in the direction of where Seth thought the edge of the wood was.

They stopped every now and again, listening for voices and to look around to see if they were being followed. Fortunately, there were no more frightening sounds of howling creatures or piercing laughter. All was quiet, and before too long they could see the daylight beyond the trees.

When they again reached the top of the vast wood, Seth looked out over the moorland. It became clear just how much it had changed from the day that he and Alice had last come over from Darwen, Alice didn't recognise any of it at all. Some of the hills seemed higher and some were of a different shape. Seth pointed out that between the time they were now in and the real time that Alice was from, there had been a huge crashing of the earth. The ground had moved and many things had changed. Seth tried to explain.

'The biggest change, and the one that has caused so much fuss, was when the earth moved, and here, all the cave entrances closed or were buried. This probably included the caves where Merlin had lived during his stay on the moors. The people of the moors had always said that, before he moved on with Arthur, Merlin had left items of great power in the cave and that these items would only be found by the person who found the five pieces of the stone. A stone he had broken and cast to the wind from the top of the Great Hill.' Seth became noticeably excited as he told Alice this tale.

'Come, we must make haste and stay safe from Bordagan.'

Seth and Alice walked, staying just inside the wood, leaving themselves enough cover so as not to be seen from the open moorland. Alice was curious to know more about Seth, how he became Dregs and if the Gatekeeper was still involved in this new time that they were now in.

Seth assured her the Gatekeeper was not involved in this treachery—nor was he involved with the last time slip he had been in, or the current time slip.

'He is from a time many years later than this, but was cursed by the same evil as me,' said Seth. Seth also wondered if it might be possible that Bordagan had heard of Alice's presence in the wood and what her purpose there was. Could this be the reason he and Alice Bond had been transported back into

Bordagan's time? Was he looking for Alice because he knew she had the stones? He found it very confusing. It was all a mystery, indeed.

They walked for a good hour and saw no one, nor heard any sounds other than the natural sounds of the birds and the light wind that blew around the tops of the trees. The wood appeared to be curving round to the right. It suddenly fell steeply and became very rocky, with some large boulders that weren't easy to scramble over. Alice struggled with these. Seth wasn't much help to her and gave her a look that as good as said, 'You're on your own.'
Alice was a woman of some fifty-odd years, and not used to climbing over such rough terrain as this, but this made no odds to Seth; he just kept going, occasionally looking back and calling to Alice to hurry along. After they had climbed and stumbled for a hundred yards or more, the rocks gave way to more forgiving land. By now, Seth was quite a way in front, but as the ground became easier, Alice soon caught up.

The lay of the land was now a downhill walk. Seth knew he was going in the right direction and the valley that lay below the wood was the end of Tockholes Wood and on the other side was the huge moor, and beyond that Brinscall Moor and Great Hill, but they had many miles of rough ground to cross yet and he had no idea how big the rest of the wood in front of them was.

Seth and Alice's attention was suddenly drawn to a commotion on the hillside to the left of the wood. They crept upwards towards the edge of the wood, staying hidden by whatever bush cover there was.

In the distance there was a large herd of deer running fast, upwards away from the wood. Seth and Alice looked back in the direction of where they had come, but they could see nothing, nor could they see anyone chasing them. They lay there and waited for a few moments.

Seth indicated to Alice that they should move on, so they got up and made their way back to the cover of the wood and continued their journey. They had not gone far when they heard voices. Seth told Alice to get down behind a bush and to be quiet.

The voices got louder. There were men, women and some children. The children were crying and the women appeared to be trying to comfort them as best they could. Seth peeped out from the bush and could count about fifteen people. They were all ordinary peasants, certainly not Bordagan's men. It was quite possible they were fleeing from the tyrant, and this was probably what had startled the deer.

Seth whispered to Alice that he was going to go and speak to them. He suggested she stay where she was and make no sound for the time being.

He stood up and called over to them, waving his hand. The men with the group raised their weapons. They were armed with bows and spears. One or two even had swords. Seth put his hands above his head and made a gesture to show that he was unarmed. He slowly made his way down through the wood towards them. They still held their weapons at the ready.

'Who are you?' they asked suspiciously. What do you want, and why are you dressed that way?'

Seth realised that he must have looked odd, as the

clothes he was wearing was from a time a thousand years later. This may have made them wonder if he was one of Bordagan's men.

'Please, fear not, I mean you no harm. I am from a far-off land, and I am making my way to Great Hill on Brinscall Moor.'

The travellers looked at Seth and asked where this Brinscall Moor was that he spoke of. It hadn't occurred to Seth that, in this time he was now in, Brinscall wasn't even a place. It hadn't been created yet. How was he going to explain this to these people?

He stuttered, and stumbled on his words.

'It is really … hmm, Great Hill that I search for, which is on a large moor; I heard the name Brinscall Moor mentioned somewhere,' spluttered Seth.

At that point, Alice stood up and began to walk down to the party. At first, the men became agitated and again raised their weapons. Then the one who seemed to be the leader of the party raised his sword and told them all to lower their arms.

'How many more of you are there?' he asked.

Alice assured him there were only the two of them and that they were nothing more than travellers. 'The hill my companion speaks of is mentioned in the land where we come from, and it is said that there will one day be a peaceful settlement built there that shall have the name Brinscall. This may only be folklore, but we do believe Great Hill exists.' The man appeared to accept Alice's explanation, and the situation calmed down.

Then Seth asked who they were and what they were so afraid of. The leader of the group told them that Bordagan had ridden into their settlement and had taken all their animals and food. Bordagan's men had killed those who tried to stop him.

'We were lucky to escape with our lives. The last we saw of our homes, was the flames that rose in the night sky.'

Seth asked where Bordagan was now and how far it was to the big moor and Great Hill.

'Why in God's name do you want to go there? There is nothing but death and destruction raging on those hills. Bordagan is looking for Arthur and the wizard Merlin, and he will stop at nothing until he finds them.'

'What of Arthur? Can he not fight back and send Bordagan packing?' asked Seth.

'Arthur is long gone, far to the north. Merlin is safe for now. His magic has hidden him deep underground. But Bordagan doesn't know this, and he believes the people of the moor are hiding him. He is searching every settlement and bothy on the hills and will stop at nothing. He slaughters all men, women and children if they stand in his way. He takes whatever he needs to feed his men and leaves nothing for those left. We cannot stay there without food throughout the winter. Do not be foolish; do not go onto those hills.'

Seth asked the man his name. 'Cedric, of Noon Hill. These are my family,' said the man.

'Where will you go now?' asked Alice.

'Over to the east, and then north to the monasteries in York. We will be safe there and fed well.'

Seth asked again how far it was to the big moor and Great Hill. The man shook his head. He said they had been travelling for half a day, a night and another half a day. He warned Seth and Alice that the land ahead was harsh and boggy with very little cover. He suggested, if they were still intent on going to Great Hill, that they should stay as close to the gullies that flowed down off the hills. He said they would help to provide some cover should they catch sight of Bordagan and his men.

The man wished Seth and Alice well, and the two parties parted in different directions. As they began to make their way further through the wood, it became colder, and the wind made it seem worse than it was as it gathered momentum.

Seth and Alice walked on, not saying a word. Each was deep in thought. Alice was lost in a mixture of thought and emotions, wondering if, how and when she would ever get back to her own time, and whether or not she would be able to deliver the stones to Squire Hoghton as planned.

For the next half a day, they followed the edge of the huge Tockholes Wood, uphill and then down, often having to climb over fallen trees and thicket that was so sharp it tore their clothes. Occasionally, they would hear the howling of wolves and the squeal of some poor wretched animal that was being torn apart as it became a meal for the savage pack.

They kept moving. Eventually, the wood became a steep descent, until they reached a brook that flowed at the very bottom of the wood. The brook was in full flow. The rain of the past few days had swelled it into a torrent. Seth said they would have to find somewhere to cross. Looking in both directions, he could see no sign of stepping stones or any makeshift bridge, but the people he had met earlier must have come that way, so he knew there must be somewhere to cross.

'I will go this way and you go that way, but not far, mind! We are safer together than alone. If you do not find anywhere beyond the bend there in the distance, come back here and we will try to find somewhere together.' His concern for her safety pleased Alice. She nodded, and they both went off in their separate directions.

Alice reached the bend and saw a bridge of sorts—two large tree trunks that were laid across the water. She turned, and went back to tell Seth what she had found. They made their way back to the bridge. Seth wondered if Alice would be capable of crossing the two trees. Alice laughed. She asked Seth to find her a long pole to help her balance. He turned away, and then realised the staffs that he had sharpened for protection would suffice.

He turned and was about to suggest she use that, but she wasn't there. Alice laughed again. She was on the other side of the brook.

'How did you get there?' asked Seth.

'I have my ways.' She laughed. 'Reach out your staff towards me and step onto the tree trunk.' As he did so, he found himself balancing perfectly smoothly, and before he knew it he was across the bridge. He stared at Alice and wondered if these powers she showed were indeed any match for Bordagan's, but somehow he doubted it. He hoped he would never be in a position to have to put them to the test, although he suspected it wouldn't trouble Alice Bond. The confidence that she exuded offered no sign of fear for anyone. The way she had stood up to the Gatekeeper had proved that.

Seth asked her where she had acquired such powers. Alice told him that it was all in his mind, and he only saw and believed what he wanted to see and believe.

'If you look into my eyes and trust what you see, That trust will keep you safe, so look deep, And you will see the power deep within me.'

Alice's rhyme sent a shiver through Seth. There was something bewitching about this strange woman whom he had met only two days before. He wondered where their adventure would take them, but he felt that it would be interesting nonetheless, and he was pleased that she was with him.

'If we are fortunate enough to find the cave where Merlin is hidden, what will you ask of him ,and how will you explain having two of the stones that he has made so special?' asked Seth.

'I cannot ask him anything about the stones, because I do not have them. If you remember, we had set off to collect the stones when this most peculiar scenario came about. How can I ask him about something that he has not yet created? She paused. But what about you, what are you going to ask of the great wizard?' Alice asked Seth.

'I want him to send me back to my own time and to free me from all spells that the Moor and the Gatekeeper have over me. I just want to live a normal life.' replied Seth.

'But we have a long way to go, and the wood looks like it still hasn't finished with us yet,' said Seth, looking upwards.

The wood stretched far up the hillside, away from the brook, and it looked like it would be a hard climb to the top, but Seth hoped that once they reached the top they would come out of the wood and onto the moor itself.

Using the staffs that Seth had made, the two of them began the long climb, each digging their staff into the ground and pulling themselves up step by step. After a while, they reached a flat rocky outcrop where they sat down and rested. The ledge was about twenty feet in length and had big jagged rocks on its edge with trees overhanging from its upper side. It was a comfortable place in a wood that at times seemed a very harsh and unwelcoming place.

Seth took out some bread from the bag he had and offered some to Alice. Alice reached in to her bag and brought out some of the cheese the innkeeper's wife had given to her. After the day's long hard trek, both of them felt weary.

Seth said it wouldn't be long before the night would be drawing in. It was by now mid-afternoon, but with the cloud above, the night would come sooner than was wanted. Looking around, Seth suggested they should remain on the flat part of the hill until morning. This worried Alice, as it would make it a long night, but Seth said he had no idea how far it was to the top of the wood and whether or not they might find a suitable enough place to rest if they carried on. Alice accepted his reasoning, and the pair of them began to put together a camp for the night.

Seth gathered some wood and proceeded to make a fire. He didn't think there would be any danger of Bordagan's men seeing them on this well hidden place so deep inside the woods. He knew the hillside would hide the light from the fire so no one on the moor would see it. His only worry was that the rising smoke might raise some suspicions, but this was a risk they would have to take. It was far too cold at night in November not to have some form of heat, and apart from that, the fire would ward off the wolf packs, should there be any around.

Once he had lit the fire, he told Alice he was going to have a look around to see what the rest of the wood looked like, and to see if he could find out how far they were from the top of the wood. He told Alice to stay close to the fire and to shout out if she needed him. Alice gave him a look that said she could more than take care of herself. He smiled, and off he went.

He had been gone no more than ten minutes when he came back proudly, holding aloft a rabbit. 'We have meat for supper tonight.' This was indeed a welcome surprise on this cold afternoon. 'And also some mushrooms and herbs that I have found. Tonight we dine like kings,' said Seth. Alice smiled, and began to build up the fire, making a spit out of wood to cook the rabbit on. Seth proceeded to skin the animal.

Darkness had fallen before the meat was cooked. Seth had also cooked the mushrooms and herbs in some leaves that he had placed on a flat stone over the fire. The juices from the rabbit also helped to cook the herbs.

It had been days since Alice and Seth had eaten so well. Seth had boiled some water in a tankard that he had in his shoulder bag, and they had a hot drink that also helped to warm them through. Feeling thoroughly full and content, it wasn't very long before the pair of them found themselves drifting off to sleep. The long hard day had clearly taken its toll on the two travellers, and although they had fallen asleep early that evening, they slept well and long, only waking occasionally when they began to shiver as the fire died down. Every now and again, one of them would wake and would place some more wood on the dying embers, and then go back to sleep again.

As day broke, they both woke to the sound of dogs barking—big dogs—and men shouting. Seth wondered if they had seen the smoke from the fire, but by now the fire was out, and even what was left was not smouldering, so there was no smell. Alice asked who they might be. Seth shook his head. He doubted they would be Bordagan's men. They were usually horsemen and had no use for dogs.

They decided they should stay where they were and make no sound or movement. The noise was coming from above them and sounded like it was a good way off. It was hard to tell if they were coming closer or moving away. They could do nothing but let events unfold.

After a short while, it sounded like the men and dogs were moving away from them. Seth asked Alice to pass him the small bag that she kept Milo in. He took the bag and shook Milo out from it.

'Again, my little one, I need your help. Go and see who and what is the danger, then show us safe passage from these woods.' Seth raised his arm and launched the small fleck of light into the woods. Milo danced for a moment and then shot off upwards away from them and out of sight. All Alice and Seth could do was wait for Milo to return. It wasn't long before the small light was back and dancing in front of Alice. She collected Milo and placed him back in the bag.

'Well, that was a lot of help; he didn't indicate where it might be safe to go,' she said.

Seth stood looking up towards where Milo had been. Then, suddenly, with a rush and great commotion, half a dozen men stood on the hill above them. Two more slid down the hill at either side of them. Seth grabbed his staff and stood ready to defend himself. Alice did the same. The men looked at them and laughed. Even Seth's size was no match for these men.

The men above aimed long bows at them, and the two men in front of them brandished swords. They had no choice but to lower their staffs.

'Who are you. What do you want with us? We are nothing more than two weary travellers.' Seth said he could tell by the way the men were dressed that they were not Bordagan's knights.

A man who looked like he was the leader jumped down from the top of the banking, and stood looking up and down at Seth and Alice.

'Where are you from? demanded the man. 'You do not dress like any travellers I have seen in these parts before,' Alice stepped forward.

'We come from far in the south and are making our way to relatives in the north.' Alice spoke again with her Devon accent. This seemed to confuse the man even more.

'Empty your bags; let me see what you have of any worth.' These comments suggested to Seth that these men were nothing more than brigands and cut-throats, looking for people to rob. They quickly turned out the contents of their shoulder bags. There was nothing more than a few items of food and some herbs that Alice had picked.

The man became agitated, and kicked the bags. He muttered something to one of his men. This worried Seth; he wondered if they might be considering killing them. Alice had other ideas. Using her powers, she stared at the bags and made them lift off the floor. The men looked on, amazed at what was happening in front of them.

The bags opened, and then Alice made stones rise from the floor and into the bags. The tops of the bags closed, and then they began to fly around and around. Then, one of the bags struck one of the men on the side of his head, and then the other felled the second man. The leader, who by now was ducking and lashing out at the bags with his sword, shouted to Alice, 'Please make them stop, I will leave you in peace if you do.' Alice dropped her gaze and the bags fell to the ground.

'Who are you? What are these powers you have? Are you Bordagan's sorcerers?' asked the frightened man.

Alice and Seth both laughed. 'No, we are no friends of Bordagan or his cut-throats, but we would like to find the wizard they call Merlin. We think he can help us to find our way to where we need to be.'

'And where would that be?' asked the leader.

Alice gave him a look that suggested he asked too many questions. 'Enough of us; who are you, and what is your name?' Seth asked.

'I am Harold of Pike Hill, and these are my men. Bordagan drove us from our homes, twenty-one nights gone. His men burnt our huts and took our livestock. Our women and children are in hiding on the great moor. We are wary of all who come this way, and we are starving. My men haven't eaten properly for days.' He called his men down from the top of the banking.

'What of this Bordagan? How long is he likely to be around here?' asked Alice.

'That is anyone's guess. He seems to follow Arthur around, but he and his men are no match for Arthur. They just wage skirmish after skirmish. Bordagan tries to impress Morgana. More fool him. He will never win that evil woman over. The only thing she desires is Arthur's crown.'

Seth told Harold he was a woodsman and a hunter. He suggested he could help his men to catch food. Harold agreed. Seth took two of the bowmen with him, and set off to go and hunt. The rest of the men relit the fire while Alice searched for herbs and wild mushrooms. The wood was full of plants that could be used, and Alice soon had a bag full of food. She also brought herbs that would heal the two men's sore heads; they were still reeling from being hit with the flying bags of stones.

After a while, the hunting party returned; they had indeed done well. There was enough food for all. There were rabbits and birds, but best of all, a young deer had been caught. Seth suggested the men should take the deer back to their women and children.

Alice set about preparing the food. As she was cooking, she thought hard, and wondered if they should tell the men the truth about where they had come from and the mystery that had befallen Seth and her. What would they make of her powers? She had no idea whether people in this strange time might accept her. She took Seth to one side and asked him what he thought, but Seth shook his head and said it was a very bad idea.

'We cannot risk telling anyone; only the great wizard Merlin should know. There are strange mysteries in this time that we are in, and people are suspicious of one another. I learned this the last time I came this way. It is too dangerous to let anyone know who we are.' Alice accepted what Seth had said, and agreed that they should continue to hide their identities.

After they had all eaten, Seth asked the men how far they were from the moor.

'No more than half a day, but you must beware—Bordagan's men are all around. They too seek the wizard. Only a handful of people know where Merlin is hidden, and they keep on the move so that Bordagan cannot torture the secret from them. If you are going onto the great moor, head over to Round Loaf Hill. There you will find some good folk who may be able to help you, but you are a long way from there yet, and many dangers are in front of you, not least Bordagan. If you meet him, tell him that you are no more than humble travellers. He will rob you; he takes everything from everyone.

He leaves them nothing. You should be grateful if you part from him with your lives,' said Harold, his men all nodding and uttering agreement.

'We will walk with you until you reach the edge of the moor, then it would be safer for you if we went our separate ways. Bordagan is hunting us, as we have taken down some of his scouts and now we are his sworn enemy, second only to Arthur,' continued Harold. The men all laughed and cheered.

Seth told Harold that they had seen Bordagan only two days before, riding through the wood. Harold nodded, saying he knew of this. His scouts had been closely following Bordagan's men. They needed to know where he was at all times, in order to stay alive.

'He was seen yesterday on the lower reaches of Belmont Moor, heading towards, Winter Hill Ridge. He has an idea where Merlin is hidden, but cannot find him, so he seeks those who do know of Merlin's whereabouts. God help them if he catches them.'

Seth kicked dirt onto the fire, putting it out. The rest of them collected their belongings together and they made their way up the hill from their rocky resting place, taking the deer with them.

Chapter 5

Slaughter on the Hills

Just as Harold had predicted, it was noon when they finally saw daylight at the edge of the wood. The moor ahead of them looked bleak and the rain that was sweeping across the hills did little to improve their plight. But there was no option, they had to move on and try to find Merlin.

'In what direction do we go?' enquired Seth. He looked completely lost. The moor in front of him was huge, open and barren, with little or no place to hide should they see Bordagan's men.

'To the south lies Winter Hill, where we last heard Bordagan was heading. To the north and west is Great Hill, but if you go straight ahead, you will eventually come to Round Loaf. That is where you should go first. There are folk there who will help you.'

Seth and Alice shook hands with the men before heading in the direction they had been told to go. They only had the word of these strangers, who they hardly knew, but something told them that they spoke the truth.

As they headed off, the small army of nine men, armed only with bows and swords, went south towards Winter Hill in pursuit of Bordagan. Their aim was to slow him down and distract him from hunting the ones who held the secret of where Merlin was. Seth wished them well.

The moor was indeed as harsh as any land Seth

or Alice had crossed before. They could expect only the wind and rain for company. No living thing would wish to inhabit this desolate land. For as far as the eye could see, there was nothing but heath and bracken and, no doubt, bogs.

The land was uphill for the next hour, and all the way up they kept looking across in the direction of Harold and his men as they made their way south. They got smaller and smaller as the two parties made their separate ways. The only good thing about the bleakness of the landscape was that they would be able to see anyone else who was on the moor, and hopefully, before they were seen.

As the cold November afternoon wore on, Alice wondered where they might rest that night. It was far too cold and wet to spend the night on the tops of the moor. It was clear they were lost, and Alice wondered if they might freeze to death before the morning. Seth said they would have no option but to keep moving, even if it meant walking right throughout the night.

The plan was to make their way to the top of one of the many high hills on the moor and hope they could see some light or smoke from a bothy, and then head towards it and ask for shelter for the night, but their hopes of finding anywhere on this godforsaken moor were bleak.

As the night moved in and light began to fade, the rain got worse. Seth saw what he thought was a cleft in the land over to the right, a few hundred yards away. He and Alice headed in that direction. The dip in the land would at least provide some protection from the wind.

They decided to rest for a while and have something to eat. There was still some rabbit left from the morning, but it was a cold meal, and they could both have done with having a hot meal inside them, but with no sign of anything to burn, there was no option. Cold meat it had to be.

After their meal, Seth stood up; his bones had become stiff after the day's, hard walk, and he knew Alice would be the same. Holding out a hand, he helped her to her feet.

'Wait there for moment I'll go and look around to see if there are any lights anywhere in view,' he said.

By now it was quite dark, and any light would stand out in the darkness. Seth climbed to the top of the cleft and looked around.

'We are in luck—yonder in the distance there are lights. It must be a settlement. It is away from the direction we want to go in, but we have no choice if we want shelter tonight.'

He jumped down, and collecting his bag, he took Alice by the hand and helped her up out of the dip. Pointing at the lights, far away in the distance, he set off, leading the way.

The ground was difficult enough to cross in the daylight. In the dark, it was treacherous. Using their staffs to steady them, they slowly made their way across the moor, heading in a downhill direction. More than once, Alice fell over, almost breaking her ankle.

Seth took her arm and helped her, until he fell into a deep bog and couldn't get out. Alice's powers were called upon again. She passed him one end of his staff and, as if she had superhuman strength, she lifted Seth out of the hole.

'If you can do that, why can you not just float us down over this wretched ground?' he asked.

'Not all things are straightforward, and my powers are only for use in times when life is in danger,' replied Alice.

Once they were organised, they were about to set off again towards the lights. As they got closer, they could hear screams and shouting coming from the direction of the lights. It wasn't long before the lights became bigger and brighter, and straight away they knew. The settlement was under attack, and the lights were of buildings burning.

'It must be Bordagan's men,' said Seth.

The piercing screams of men and women suggested people were being slaughtered down there. All Alice and Seth could do was lie on the ground, watch and wait. The mayhem seemed to go on for half an hour. As the flames rose higher into the night, the screaming became less frequent.

They wondered if anyone had survived the attack, but they didn't dare move for fear of being seen. Seth said it was best to wait until all was quiet. He put his ear to the ground to listen for the sound of horses riding away. There it was, and the sound was becoming louder. The horses were coming in their direction.

Alice suggested they run back to the cleft at the top of the hill, but Seth said there wasn't time and it was too far and too dangerous. All they could do was lie still and hope they wouldn't be seen in the darkness. As the riders passed them, they were able to count around thirty riders.

They were in luck; the horsemen rode past them. They were no more than a few feet away. Thankfully, the dark night and the long grass gave them protection. Alice and Seth waited until Seth could hardly hear the sound of hooves on the ground before they got up and made their way down the hill to the burning settlement. The path the horsemen had taken was along a track. Seth was glad they hadn't found the track earlier, or they could have been right in their path.

As they got nearer, the carnage became clearer. The sound of people weeping was everywhere. Some were shouting for help and others were running around, trying to put out fires. There were people lying on the ground. Some were dead and some badly injured. Women were crying over the bodies of their menfolk. Their children were in shock. Some just stood there, staring into the night.

There was one man who was hopelessly fetching one bucket at a time from the stream at the side of the village and throwing the water onto the flames of his bothy. His feeble efforts made no difference. When Alice suggested he stop, that it was useless, he told her his wife and child were inside. The house was barely standing, but still, the man kept fetching water.

Alice had never seen such destruction or murderous loss of life before. Seth said he had witnessed similar to this before by Bordagan and his men. He had seen it the last time he was in the time slip. That was how he knew of Bordagan's evil.

All that night, the two of them stayed and helped

to dress the wounds of the injured and to bury the dead. When daylight arrived, the destruction became even more visible. Bordagan's men hadn't bothered to make off with the animals as they had in the past; they had just killed them all for the sake of it, and set fire to the carcases.

An elderly man had taken charge of the camp and was, in a gentle way, telling people what needed to be done. He said they had no means of food left. The grain that had been stored in one of the buildings was burned, and with the animals dead, they had no milk or meat.

Seventy-four people had lived in this settlement before Bordagan had called that night. Twelve were dead, nearly all menfolk, and twenty-six injured, some very badly. None of the villagers noticed the different way that Alice and Seth were dressed. No one asked questions. Some thanked them for their help. After the last of the dead had been buried, it was decided that the survivors would have to move on to stay with relatives.

Makeshift stretchers were put together on which the more seriously injured were laid, and the stronger of the menfolk carried them over the rough ground. There was, thankfully, a cart track leading away from the settlement. Seth asked where it went.

'It goes to Noon Hill and the valleys beyond,' said one of the women. "Bordagan won't go there, to the Noon. There is a darkness about the place. Many years ago, it was said Satan lived on the hill, and the lives of young women were offered up to him to appease his thirst for blood. Bordagan knows of this tale and is afraid of the hill, but members of my family have dwelled there for many generations. It is true there is a strange presence around the hill, but no one has ever come to any harm, not that we would tell Bordagan that.'

Noon Hill was in the wrong direction from where Seth and Alice needed to go. They told the settlers that they had to head over to Great Hill, and asked how far it was. They gasped on hearing this.

'You will be in grave danger going over there. Bordagan's men are crawling all over that side of the moor. Many have fled from there and made their way to the Noon, or to Round Loaf. You have witnessed the fate that has befallen us, and we have done nothing to him. You will surely not survive if you go there.' They pleaded with Seth and Alice to reconsider, but they knew it was the only chance they had of unravelling the mystery and magic that had engulfed them in Tockholes wood. It had to be done!

They didn't tell them the purpose of their mission, only that it was of great importance so much so that, if successful, it may rid the moor of Bordagan for good. The elder told them that, if they were lucky, they could reach Great Hill in a day, but with Bordagan and his men swarming all over the place, it would probably take them longer.

'If you head north first before you reach the hill, you will find a farmstead belonging to Will Strong. God willing, he has not been a victim of Bordagan's bloodletting. Will is a good man and knows Great Hill, well. He will guide you. Tell him Cuthbert of Noon sent you, and tell him what has happened here.' Seth and Alice shook hands with Cuthbert and bid farewell to them all.

The directions Cuthbert had given them meant they had to go back over the hill from which they had come the day before. They stood and watched as the sad party moved off, carrying their wounded with them. Just a few trails of smoke were still rising from the settlement.

Alice looked at the fresh mounds of earth where they had buried the dead. Sadness overcame her and she wiped the tears from her eyes before following Seth up the hill. For a woman who had herself been party to misdoings that had caused sadness to others, this was indeed a new feeling, and she wasn't normally the sort who allowed her feelings to show.

Within the hour they were over the top of the hill and down the other side. At the bottom of the hill they reached a gully, turned left and were heading towards the north. There was no sign of any settlements, not even a solitary bothy anywhere in sight. The day was cold and rain threatened, although it had stayed dry thus far. The ground over which they had to travel was uneven, to say the least. Large tufts of heather covered much of the moor, and where there was no heather to contend with, there were marshlands and deep bogs.

The view from the hills was amazing; they could see right out to the coast. They could also see the smoke from the houses in Priest-town on the banks of the River Ribble. This was a large settlement, made up mainly of Celtic monks. These monks were part of the Melrose sect. Some said they were quite warrior-like and feared no one. Priest-town had grown since the days of the Roman rule and had become independent.

After travelling for half a day, Alice said she needed to stop. The harsh ground conditions had taken their toll on Alice's feet; her shoes were soaking wet and the leather had rubbed the skin from her toes. She was in considerable pain and needed to bandage them with some dry cloth from her petticoat.

While they rested, Alice asked Seth about his other personality, Dregs. She wanted to know if he could still change himself from one to the other. Her idea was that if he could, it might help them in some way. But Seth shook his head.

'You forget, we are not in the time when I was cursed with this spell, so I am here as I am,' he replied.

'Have you tried?' asked Alice.

'There is no point. How can it possibly work if it was from another time?'

'Well, my little magic trick worked the other day when you fell into that bog and couldn't get out, so what is the difference?' retorted Alice.

Seth looked at her and wondered if she might be right. Then he took a deep breath and began to bend over. A deep grunt came from him as he fell to his knees. He became twisted and gnarled, moaning as he writhed before her. Alice looked on. She knew it was working, but at the same time she found it a very unerving experience. After only a few moments, Seth stood up, but now he was Dregs, bent and with his face covered in warts, and with his hair long, unkempt and dirty.

'Woman, you were right,' he grunted.

Alice laughed, and clapped her hands. Then she asked him to turn himself back again.

'Make up your mind, woman.' Dreg's voice was that of a bad-tempered man, not like the caring Seth, who he had been a few minutes earlier, but this didn't concern Alice.

Dregs reversed the process and was soon standing upright, tall and stronge—the man Alice had come to trust.

'You were right. I didn't think it would work, but that is good, it might help us in some way if we need help,' said Seth.

Alice was by now all bandaged up, and happy to proceed onwards to find the farmstead of Will Strong. The hillside they were following had a few twists and turns before falling away steeply into a ravine. At the bottom of the ravine, there was the farmstead that belonged to Will Strong. There was smoke rising from the stack, but no sign of anyone around.

As they approached, a huge dog came from the back of the cottage and barked furiously at them. It didn't make any attempt to attack them, but made enough noise to bring out the occupants. Two men emerged, brandishing swords and shields. Both of them were wrapped in sack cloth and had large wolfskin capes around their shoulders. This made them appear larger than they were. Seth recognised them to be Saxons. He raised his hands, indicating that he and Alice meant them no harm.

'We come as friends; we mean you no harm. Cuthbert of Noon sent us to seek you out,' said Seth.

The two men looked at one another and lowered their swords.

'What news of Cuthbert?' asked one of the men.

'Which one of you is Will Strong?' asked Seth. Alice was happy for Seth to do the talking.

'I am Will Strong,' said the man. Now what of Cuthbert? Why has he sent you here?'

Seth told the man of the slaughter at the settlement and how they had come across it as it was unfolding. They told Will that men, women and even children had died and been wounded there the night before, and how they were almost ridden over by Bordagan's men as they rode away.

Will took Seth and Alice inside and gave them a hot drink and some hot broth. This was most welcome. It was the first hot food they had had for two days. The fire in the middle of the room was soon put to good use as Will's wife took their clothes and laid them over a clothes horse to dry them.

Will asked many questions about Cuthbert, and did they know who had died and who had survived, but Seth and Alice were unable to give them the information they asked for. Will explained that his sister and two of his cousins lived in the settlement. Alice reassured him, saying that if any harm had befallen them, surely Cuthbert would have said so.

This made sense to Will. Then he asked about Bordagan, wanting to know where he had gone, but Seth shook his head. All he could tell him was that he had ridden east and that the day before he had been seen heading towards Winter Hill. Seth also told him of the meeting they had had with Harold of Pike Hill and his small band of men, and of how they had gone off to the east, following Bordagan.

'Harold is a fool if he thinks he can outwit Bordagan. He had the chance to join us, but instead he chose to take on Bordagan on his own with his small band of men. They are only crofters who have no experience of fighting a devil like Bordagan. This choice was made after Bordagan burned their settlement to the ground. It is his choice,' said Will, shaking his head.

Suddenly there was a noise, and the floor behind them moved. A wooden trapdoor with a mat covering it lifted. A hole appeared, and four more men climbed out of the hole. Alice and Seth looked on in astonishment. They couldn't believe what they saw.

Will and the other man helped the men up, and introduced them to Alice and Seth. He told the men what he had been told about the attack on the settlement.

He could see that Alice and Seth were intrigued by the hole in the floor, and he explained to them what was going on. Before this, Alice and Seth had already told him about their mission to find the hidden cave of Merlin, but they hadn't mentioned anything of whom they were or where they were from.

'The hole, you see, leads deep into a network of caves and tunnels that go far underneath the entire moor. They twist and turn for miles. We still haven't been through them all, there are far too many. They are where we hide and strike out at Bordagan,' said Will.

'Does this tunnel lead to where the wizard Merlin

hides?' asked Alice.

'If it does, we haven't found him. He is in a cave that is known only to him and a chosen few. Some of the people of the moor think they know where the entrance to his cave is, but it can't be seen or entered. They leave food for him at certain points, and the following day it is gone, but he has never been seen taking it,' Will told them.

'We need to find him; it is very important,' said Seth..

Will became suspicious, and demanded to know why it was so important. Alice asked Will if she could have a moment alone outside with Seth. Will was now unsure about these two strangers and their motives. He wondered if they were spies for Bordagan, but he nodded and allowed them to have their moment.

Once outside, Alice again suggested they should tell Will and his men the truth about who they were and where they had come from. Seth thought she was mad, but she assured Seth that it was their best hope of getting Will to help them. She convinced Seth that they had their own brand of magic and spells that could keep them safe and maybe even persuade Will that they could help him in his fight against Bordagan, as long as he would help them.

Seth reminded Alice what he had told her only two days before when she had suggested this, but she was adamant that it was their best hope. Seth reluctantly agreed.

When they went inside, they were met by all six men, who were now holding their swords and looking as if they were ready to use them, if necessary. Two of the men moved behind Seth and Alice and blocked the doorway. The mood had now become quite hostile.

Will Strong told the two of them to sit down and start talking.

'I want the truth from you, or I'll cut you from ear to ear and feed you to the dogs. Now, who are you? You do not dress like folk from these parts, nor do you speak the same way. I suspect you are Bordagan's spies.' The men then became very agitated, and Alice knew they needed to talk fast, or the situation could well become nasty.

'Very well. I doubt you will believe what I am about to say to you, but I assure you that what I am about to say is the truth,' said Alice. 'My name is Alice Bond, and this man is known only as Seth. We come from a time many years ahead, from a time where Arthur and Merlin are only writings in history books. Many kings have ruled since Arthur. And it is a time where mine and Seth's magic dictates.'

Alice told them of the journey she was making, and of the magic runes of Merlin. She told them of her meeting with the Gatekeeper, and how Bordagan had played his part throughout all this time. Seth said Merlin was their only hope of ever ridding their time of Bordagan and bringing peace to Tockholes wood.

Will didn't believe them. He told them to prove their magic, and if they could, he would let them live. Alice said, 'Very well, if that is what it takes.' She stood and outstretched her arms. She lowered her head and began to mumble something strange. In an instant, the tips of the men's swords fell to the ground, and no matter how hard they tried, they couldn't lift them off the floor. Some tried using both hands.

'What kind of sorcery is this?' asked one of the men.

'You asked me to prove my powers to you, so there you are,' she replied.

But they also couldn't lift their swords, now they couldn't free their hands from them Alice walked freely around the room. None of the men could do anything to stop her.

'What we have told you is the truth; we are not any part of Bordagan's band. We seek only to find Merlin, as we said. If I were your enemy, I could finish you all now, but that is not my aim. If you will join with us and help us find the secret cave of Merlin, we will help you in your fight against Bordagan.' Alice stopped speaking, and released the spell she was holding them with.

Each and every one of them was stunned by what had just happened. They lifted their swords with ease and looked at them, and then at each other.

'You have great powers, so why didn't you stop Bordagan's men last night when they were slaughtering our kinfolk?' asked Will.

'When the fighting started, we were too far away and we were not sure what was happening. It was only as we got nearer to the village that we became aware of the carnage. By then it was too late, and the damage had been done,' said Seth

Will agreed that he and his men would help Seth and Alice as much as they could, but he made it clear that no one had any idea where Merlin was or how to find him. Seth asked if any of the tunnels might lead to Great Hill and the cave where Merlin was hidden.

'I doubt it. There is a deep valley that runs between Round Loaf and Great Hill. There is one tunnel that seems to lead down that way, but we don't go there. Many of the men that have dared to enter the cavern have not returned. There is a large lagoon in a cavern at the bottom of that tunnel, and the water in that lagoon is blacker than the night sky. Strange sounds come from the cavern; sounds that are not made by any form of man that I know of. I have been down there only once. I was glad to get out. I am not sure that there is any way out of the cavern other than the way we enter from, but my men will not go there. You enter that place at your own peril,' said Will.

'You are safer trying to find Merlin from the top of Great Hill, even with Bordagan and his men hunting you down,' said another.

Alice and Seth needed time to think. Will suggested they rest there for the night and consider what to do the following day. The light was by this time beginning to fade. Night came fast on these November afternoons. Will told his wife to make beds up for his guests. Some of the other men still seemed unconvinced of the sincerity of Seth and Alice's story. Alice could tell this by the looks they gave and by the way they whispered to each other.

Seth had also picked up on this, and quietly said to Alice that he thought it strange that there was only one woman and no children. The farmstead was easily big enough to house more than one family. Will Strong must have guessed what they were thinking.

'You must be wondering where our women folk and children are. They are living deep underground in one of the caverns. I will go there tonight and speak with our leader.'

'I thought you were the leader,' said Seth

'No, our leader is the king of all the Saxons of South Western Northumbria, and his name is Aldfrid. He is gathering an army to fight all these invaders of our lands, and that includes Arthur and Bordagan. But Bordagan is the worst. He butchers our people at will. Aldfrid tries to raise his army, but Arthur has already taken most of the fighting men for his battle against Morgana,' said Will.

'What of Merlin? Where does he stand in all this chaos? asked Seth.

'Aldfrid has no quarrel with Merlin, even though he is Arthur's man. He will give safe passage to Merlin. Aldfrid is not a butcher, he is an honourable man who wants only peace for his people. I will go and tell him what you have told me. I will be back by first light.'

That night, Seth and Alice hardly slept. Both of them had a feeling of unease. Neither of them was sure they had been believed, and for all that Will Strong and his men had said about this King of the Saxons, and how honourable a man he was meant to be, they both knew that their story would be hard for anyone to believe.

All through the night, one man or another would get up from time to time to change watch and to put more wood on the fire. The night went without any trouble, but by dawn Seth and Alice were incredibly tired. The whole house was awoken by the sound of the trapdoor to the tunnel opening. It was Will and two more men returning.

Seth thought Will might have brought his king back with him, but there was no sign of Aldfrid. When they were all up, Will turned to Seth and Alice.

'We know you have strong powers, and I have told Aldfrid what you told us, but he didn't believe me. He wants to meet you for himself … I expected he would. We will travel through the tunnels to meet him, as it will be too dangerous to go over land, although it would be quicker. We will eat and then we leave.'

Alice and Seth looked at one another. They didn't have much choice. Seth asked Will about his hopes and plans of finding Merlin.

'Will your king help us to find Merlin? Does he know where he is?' asked Seth.

Will made it clear that any decisions about such things would have to come from Aldfrid himself. He did, however, try to assure the two of them that Aldfrid was their best hope, but first they would have to convince the King that they were good people with good intentions. He said that Aldfrid found it hard to trust anyone except those very close to him. He assured Seth and Alice that, if they were to find Merlin, going through the tunnels was far better than going over land where Bordagan's men were.

Will Strong wondered what Aldfrid would make of these two strangers. Their hair was dark brown, not fair like the Saxon, and their clothes and boots resembled none that they had seen before. And they spoke so differently that he could hardly understand a word they said; how would Aldfrid understand them?

Once they had eaten, the party made ready to leave. Will told Alice and Seth that the way through the tunnels wasn't an easy path. There would be times when the tunnel became quite low and they would have to crawl on hands and knees, but he did assure them it would be dry, although that didn't worry Alice much.

Her main concern was that time was running out, and she wouldn't be able to deliver the stones to Cedric Hoghton. Mistress Preston had told her she only had four days in which to get to his house. Alice wondered what the consequences would be. Seth, on the other hand, was worried about meeting Aldfrid. He didn't think the Saxon king would believe what he and Alice had to tell him.

Will helped Alice down the ladder into the tunnel, followed by Seth and three of Will's men. Each one of them carried torches to light the way. The climb down was easy; it led down some steps into the first section which was high and opened up into a cavern.

The passage through the tunnels did, as Will had said, take a lot of twists and turns, with some easy large walkways and others that were not so pleasant, but overall it wasn't too bad. Alice did have to crawl at times, and this was hard, with her long clothes and heavy cape. She turned to Seth and suggested he should make himself into Dregs where it became narrow and low, but Seth would have none of it.

He said it would be better to hold on to that as a surprise in case they needed it later. Alice realised what he meant, and agreed with him.

They had been walking and crawling for about an hour when Will stopped them. He pointed forward.

'Just around yonder bend we will pass a tunnel to the right of us. Down that passage there lies the dark lagoon that I told you of. Do not be tempted to go down there; some have, and have not been seen again.' With that he waved them all forward.

As they reached the entrance to the tunnel he had warned them about, they stopped. It was as black as pitch, and there were some very strange noises to be heard. Will said it was the spirits of those who had gone down there and never returned. He said they could always be heard moaning—lost souls, gone forever into the bowels of Satan's hell.

Alice thought the description was a little dramatic, but nonetheless, the sounds did not play kindly to the ear, and with that the party quickly moved on. After the dark tunnel, the passage took a sharp turn to the left and began to climb. There were many other offshoots along the way. It was indeed a labyrinth, and one could easily have become lost.

Before too long, they could hear voices. Will told them it was because they were nearing the cavern where Aldfrid and the men were. As they approached, they were met by guards on the edge of one of the passageways. They saluted with their spears as Will passed them. This made Seth wonder just how high-ranking Will Strong was in Aldfrid's court.

Once inside the huge chamber, Alice looked

around. Torches and braziers lit the cavern and people were busying themselves—men and women, as well as children. All were involved in some task or other. Over by one wall of the cavern was a massive stash of weapons, enough for a hundred men or more. Aldfrid was certainly amassing an army.

But what was his intention? wondered Seth. Was it to fight Bordagan, or Arthur? Surely he wasn't a match for either. Bordagan was hunting Arthur, so he must have a force large enough to be reckoned with, and nobody had any idea what size of an army Arthur would return with on his way back south. Seth spoke to Alice of his concerns. Alice said she hoped they could find their way back to their own time before these armies met one another, and Seth agreed.

Will led them into the cavern and took them over to a table, where they sat and were given food and drink. It was the children who waited on them, some of them giving curious looks at the two strangers dressed in odd clothes. In fact, they couldn't help but notice that they were being watched by everyone.

'Pay no attention to them,' said Will. They are just wary of all strangers, especially those who dress differently from us,' then. He smiled.

This relaxed the pair somewhat, and they ate their meal. Alice noticed the smoke rising from the fires and then disappearing into the roof of the cavern. She wondered where it went, and allowed her curiosity to get the better of her. She asked one of the women close by.

'How does the smoke escape from in here? Where

does it go to?' she asked.

The woman looked at Alice. She had difficulty in understanding her. Eventually, she grasped what Alice meant, and explained that it escaped naturally out through cracks in the rocks above.

'Is that not dangerous? Will Bordagan not see the smoke and come to investigate?' asked Alice.

The woman told her that they had once captured one of Bordagan's men, and he had told them that Bordagan had seen the smoke and thought it was the hill on fire; he believed it to be the earth smouldering, ready to erupt. He said that Bordagan was a very superstitious man and avoided places that he thought had connections with evil spirits, such as Round Loaf and Noon Hill.

Alice asked where Bordagan's man was now. She was told he had been given to the women of Noon, and the least said of him, the better. Alice got the impression she might be asking too many questions, so she put her head down and carried on eating.

Right in the centre of the cavern was a huge rock that reached almost up to the roof. It must have been a good forty feet high and equally as round. Against one side of the rock was a throne. This must have been for Aldfrid, thought Alice; only a king would sit on a seat such as that.

Alice and Seth both looked around, trying to see this man who was the king of the Saxons, but everyone looked ordinary. No one seemed to have any air of authority, apart from Will. Seth called over to Will. 'When will we meet this king of yours?' he asked. Time is important to us.'

'Soon—he will be here soon. He has been over

to Noon Hill. I told him what you told me. He has gone to speak with those who were there on that night, he won't be long now.' This put their minds at ease.

After they had eaten, Will took them around the cavern, showing them the men as they did their fighting training, and they saw others making weapons such as bows and arrows, and spears. The womenfolk made clothes and shoes, and cooked. The children fetched and carried as was required; everyone played a part. There were carcases of animals hanging, ready to be butchered and prepared for meals. Large ovens baked bread, and tables were piled high with vegetables and herbs.

It was a most impressive sight to see so much going on in this vast underground hideout. In every nook and cranny there was something happening. There were also tunnels leading out of the cavern, and people came and went from them all the time.

Will explained to Seth and Alice that most of these people were Saxon, but some were Celts who had become caught up in the troubles. They had joined Aldfrid because they saw that he was trying to bring peace.

Suddenly, drums began to beat, and the noise was deafening. It was obvious that this meant Aldfrid was approaching. Will led them back to the tables and sat them down, but told them to stand when Aldfrid entered. Then horns blew and everyone stood.

In marched around twenty men followed by Aldfrid, who was followed by more men. Once they were in the cavern, the drums fell silent, as did the horns. Aldfird was a big man, a true leader and a fighter Will approached him and bowed. Aldfrid touched Will on his shoulder and the two of them walked off, talking. It was clear that Will Strong was high up in Aldfrid's estimation; indeed, they seemed more like good friends than king and servant.

Alice and Seth sat down again as life seemed to return to normal. Everyone carried on doing what they had been doing. Aldfrid and Will disappeared out of sight as they walked around the far side of the huge rock. All the two of them could do was wait. Alice's patience was by now wearing thin, and all she could think of was finding a way back to her own time.

She asked Seth how he had found his way back the last time he was in the time slip. Seth said it had happened all by itself; he said he couldn't remember how it had happened, but it just did. Maybe it would be the same this time. Alice wanted to know how long he had been trapped the last time. Again, he said he couldn't remember. She was by now getting very agitated, so Seth told her to calm down.

Just then, one of Aldfrid's men summoned them to follow him. At last, thought Alice.

Chapter 6

Aldfrid

Alice picked up her shoulder bag and followed Seth and Aldfrid's man. They went around the huge rock and then down one of the many tunnels that led off from the cavern. This led into another smaller cavern that was Aldfrid's private chamber. Will was there waiting for them, along with the King and a group of others.

Will beckoned them forward. Aldfrid had by this time changed, and Seth and Alice could see his face much more clearly than when he had walked in through the main cavern. His hair was fair and long, his beard the same. He sat back in his chair and stared at the pair. He said nothing for a few moments, and just stared as if he was trying to make something of them. This agitated Seth and he attempted to speak, but Will took a step forward and told him to hold his tongue.

'No one speaks without being asked to,' said Will.

Aldfrid raised his hand as if to say it was all right. Will stepped back. This change of tone from Will unnerved Seth and Alice. They looked at one another. Then Aldfrid spoke.

'So, I am told you have amazing magic powers and that you are looking for the wizard Merlin. I am intrigued to know why you seek a wizard if you already have such powers of your own. Will tells me that you have demonstrated your powers to him. I would like to see an example of these powers,' said the King.

'Very well,' said Alice. She turned, looked at one of the two guards who were standing by the side of Aldfrid. He was holding a long spear in his hand. Staring straight at him, she mumbled something. Suddenly, the spear jolted from his grasp and fell to the ground. Alice muttered something else, and the spear transformed itself into a snake and writhed around on the floor. Then Alice stepped forward and bent down. As she grabbed hold of the snake, it immediately turned back into a spear. She handed it back to the stunned guard, and stood back by Seth's side.

'And what of you? What can you do that would have any bearing upon your claims of magic?' asked the King.

Seth looked at Alice and then whispered something to her. Aldfrid asked what he was whispering for. Seth told the King that he had only one magic trick that he could show him, and wondered if it might be inappropriate to perform it in such important company.

'Whatever it is, you will not make me afraid, so let us see your magic trick.'

Seth nodded and stepped forward. He looked down at the floor and concentrated. His body jolted, and he fell to his knees and began to moan. His whole body became twisted and deformed. The moaning became louder and then stopped. Seth had now become Dregs once again. He stood and looked at the King.

'Well, Your Majesty, see what I have become. This was cursed upon me by Bordagan, not in this time. In a time much later—hundreds of years later,'

Dregs began to dance around, and laughed out loud.

'Enough,' said the King. 'I have seen enough. This is not magic; it is evil, and has no place here. There is no way your twisted claims of magic can be of any help to our cause.' As he spoke, Dregs changed back to Seth again.

'But …' Alice was about to protest when Will interrupted.

'Silence! Demanded Will, I told you to speak only when asked.' The two guards now stood ready with spears outstretched, and more men came into the chamber. Aldfrid said he didn't believe the story of coming from another time. He thought it to be just an excuse.

'I am sure you are nothing more than sorcerers, and I wonder if it is Arthur or Bordagan who has sent you here. Are you part of the plot to gain our lands? Is this tale of trying to find the wizard Merlin just a part of the plot to seek us out and learn of our strengths?'

Aldfrid said. 'I will sleep before I decide what to do about you. You will come to no harm here, but beware; if you attempt to use your sorcery to bring harm to anyone here, you will pay dearly. Take them away.' Aldfrid had spoken, and Seth and Alice decided not to argue. It would serve no purpose. That night they were well fed well and given beds, and fur pelts to keep them warm. As they settled down, they talked. Both wondered what fate Aldfrid would have waiting for them the following morning.

The night was a long one. Neither of them slept much. Their thoughts were taken up by wondering what their fate would be. The cavern was busy all night with men coming and going, people stoking the braziers and women cooking and baking bread. How anyone slept in all this commotion was beyond Alice.

Seth must have eventually fallen asleep, because he was woken by Alice shaking him. There were a lot of people gathering, and food was being served. It must have been breakfast time. A woman came over to them and asked if they wanted some food. She said they would have to eat where they were, because the others didn't trust them. Word had spread that they were Arthur's or Bordagan's spies.

Alice and Seth assured her they weren't. They both thanked the woman and she brought their food over to them. Alice ate some and then put the rest in her bag. Seth did the same. Neither of them knew what the day had in store for them, but they suspected it wouldn't be to their favour. Not long after they had finished eating, two guards came and told them the King would see them now. They collected their belongings and followed the two men back to the chamber where they had seen Aldfrid the day before.

The entire chamber was full of men, all armed with spears and swords. Some even had bows ready. Seth and Alice felt very uneasy and feared for their lives. They stepped forward in front of the King. Will Strong was again at Aldfrid's right hand, and looking very stern.

'Last night,' began the King, 'I slept well, but I had a vision, a warning! I was told to beware of you, woman. I was warned that you are not who you say you are. I know now that you are from another place, but whether that place is in another time, I do not know. My vision was true and the message very clear. You are not to be trusted.' He looked at Seth and told him not to trust his companion.

'This woman is dangerous. I know that you too are from another place, but your affliction is by another's magic. I now have to consider what to do with you both,' said Aldfrid.

Two chairs were brought forward and placed behind Seth and Alice. The guards indicated to them to sit, while Aldfrid went away with Will Strong and two others. After a short while they returned. Alice and Seth stood again.

'When you came to the farmstead of Will Strong, you gave him a story of helping some of our folk who had been attacked by Bordagan and his brigands. Will sought out Cuthbert to seek the truth of what had happened and to learn of your involvement. Cuthbert confirmed your story and told Will that he had sent you in good faith to his house. Because of this, I am going to let you go free, but you will receive no further help from us. I trust my vision, and my vision was not to trust you. You can take some food with you, but do not come to us again for assistance. You must take your chances against Bordagan. Your evil and your sorcery may be enough to protect you,' said Aldfrid as he looked straight at Alice. Then he again warned Seth to beware of her. Alice protested, and shouted out that the King was wrong about her.

'Sire, your vision was nothing more than a bad dream.' She admitted she did have magic, but her magic was only for good use. The King waved her away; he was having none of it. The guards led them out of the chamber.

Once they were back in the main cavern, Will Strong came to them and assured them they would have safe passage and be given food and warm clothing. He said they should be grateful that Aldfrid was a compassionate man and had been prepared to listen to his words and to Cuthbert's version of events. If he had been a bad man, he would not have listened and they would be being fed to the dogs by now. Alice and Seth both knew they could do nothing to change the King's mind. They would just have to take their chances with Bordagan.

The old woman, who had earlier brought them food, returned again with food for their journey and also some long, warm, wolfskin pelts. Alice looked at the skins and grimaced.

'Take them; you will be glad of these in the coming days. The weather on these hills is a friend to nobody. If you don't get killed by Bordagan, the cold will finish you off,' said the woman, laughing as she handed the clothing to them.

Will Strong and six of his men escorted the pair back down the passageway and away from Aldfrid's hideaway. They saw nothing more of the King that day. After a half a day of walking and crawling through the passages, they finally arrived back at the steps that led up to the inside of Will Strong's cottage. They had stopped only briefly on the way back, and that was at the dark tunnel that led down to the black cavern. The strange noises that they had heard on the way in were still there.

Will knocked on the wooden trapdoor, and it was

lifted from above by one of Will's men. The party climbed up into the room one by one. No one spoke a word. It was as if they all knew what the outcome of their meeting with Aldfrid was. Only Will had anything to say.

'We have treated you well, as you know. Tell no one of this place or of Aldfrid. Go from here, and may peace be with you.' Will's words surprised Alice. She thought he might have been more forceful and unkind. Seth stretched out his hand and shook hands with Will.

Alice did the same, but Will declined her offer, and she withdrew it disappointedly. It made her wonder what Aldfrid had seen in his vision that could have shown her in such a terrible light.

The door to the farmhouse opened, and the pair walked out. The old woman had not been wrong. It was a bitterly cold wind that blew. Rain was threatening, and as they looked around, there was no sign of a bothy or hut anywhere in sight.

Seth looked upwards trying to make out where the sun lay in the sky. He wondered how much more of the day was left, and where they could seek shelter for the coming night. Alice looked all around, but all she could see was bleak wilderness. There was just wild moorland, with nothing and no one around. The view from where they stood stretched for miles. They turned back once more to look towards Will Strong's house, but they couldn't see it. A heavy mist had come down and had covered the whole of the valley behind them.

'Strange things are happening here,' said Alice. Seth agreed.

'We should go. We will find our bearings from the top of yonder hill,' said Seth, he   pointed towards some high ground nearby.

Chapter 7

The Old Woman of the Hills

The two of them set off, making their way to the rise that Seth had pointed out. It didn't take long to reach the top. There were quite a lot of rocks on top of the hill, big and small. The larger ones helped to provide shelter from the howling November wind. Seth commented on this, but his words caused Alice to question whether it was November, as she wondered if such a month even existed in these dark times.

Seth looked around to see if there was any sign of civilisation. At first he couldn't see anything, and then in the distance, in the middle of a small copse, a puff of smoke rose out of the treetops.

'Look, over there … Smoke!' Alice stood, and saw it too. A great sense of relief overcame her. With some luck they wouldn't have to spend the night out in the open.

'Come, it will take us a good hour to reach that copse, and darkness won't be far behind us by then,' said Seth, taking hold of Alice's hand and dragging her like a doll.   Using their staffs for support, they made their way down off the hillside in the direction of the copse, which was quite a way off. The ground on those hills was rough and full of large tufts of grass and heather. There were muddy bogs that occasionally caught them out as one or the other slipped into them. A stranger walking alone over those hills would have no chance if they fell into one of the bogs. Some were quite deep, and the mud was freezing cold.

Alice struggled when Seth accidentally slipped into one. It was only when she called upon her powers to give her extra strength that she was able to get him out. Seth was again grateful. He couldn't understand what Aldfrid had meant when he said he should beware of this woman. If she had meant him harm, why would she help him like that?

After walking for some time, they found themselves on the edge of a gully. It was a water channel that carried the rainwater off the hills and down to the valleys below. There was water running down it, but not too much.

The gully seemed to follow a path towards the copse where the smoke was coming from. Seth's thoughts of it only taking them an hour to reach the copse were wrong. The harsh ground and falling into bogs had hampered them. The afternoon was drawing in fast when they finally reached the small wood. The gully became more of a stream as it reached the trees. Luckily, there was a place to cross where someone had placed stones in the water, creating a bridge.

There it was, the place where the smoke was coming from. It was a broken-down old cottage with half its roof caved in. There was no sign of life to suggest it might be a permanent dwelling for someone. All around it, the ground was even and covered in grass.

Alice had a bad feeling about this place; she sensed that all was not good. Seth made his way to the door, if that was what it could be described as. It was no more than a few boards of wood crudely put together, and looked as if it was just propped up to help keep out the wind and rain.

Seth knocked. He knocked again, but no one answered. Alice suggested that maybe the occupant was out somewhere on the moor, going about their business. Seth knocked again, louder, and called out.

'Hello! Is there anyone here?'

Again, no answer, so Seth pushed the door open. It almost fell inwards to the ground; he just managed to catch it, and propped it up against the wall. He and Alice cautiously stepped inside. There was nobody there, but there was a welcoming fire blazing away in a stone hearth and a large pile of logs stacked alongside the wall. The far end of the room had collapsed where the roof had fallen in. A poor attempt had been made to shutter it off with boards, and to keep out the cold and the wet with sackcloth. Although crudely done, it did work. The rest of the room was warm and dry.

There was a seat and a bed of sorts. Alice sat on the seat as Seth locked the door. He looked around to see if there might be some clues as to who lived in this place, but there was little to suggest it could be more than one person, and he had no idea if that one person was a man or a woman.

By the hearth there was a cooking pot and one plate and a cup. There was fresh meat and some birds hanging from hooks by the side of the wall. There was also a large bowl of herbs and vegetables. Whoever this person was, they had no intention of going hungry.

'I suspect whoever lives here will return before darkness falls. We must be on our guard; they may not take lightly to our intrusion,' said Seth. Alice agreed.

As they sat quietly, listening for footsteps from outside, there was a loud sneeze. It came from behind the boards and sacking by the collapsed roof. Seth and Alice shot to their feet.

'Who's there? Come out now!' demanded Seth. 'We mean you no harm,' said Seth as he grabbed his staff for protection. Alice stood behind him, wondering what to expect.

No one came out, but there was a sound of shuffling from behind the boards. Seth stepped forward and took hold of the sacking that hung down from the roof beams. He gave it a huge tug and down it came, along with some of the boards.

Huddled in the corner under a large wooden table was the figure of an old woman. She had her back to them and was curled up as if she feared for her life.

'Come out. It's alright, woman; we do not mean you any arm,' said Seth.

The woman shook her head vigorously but made no attempt to turn around or come out. Seth again tried to reassure her that they would not harm her, but the woman wouldn't turn around.

'If you don't come out of there, I will come and get you out. You cannot stay there all night. What are you afraid of?' he asked her.

'It is not I who should be afraid, but you. I am unclean, and you will be too if you come near me,' said the woman. Then she turned and faced them. They could just make out her face in the poor firelight. At first, it appeared she had some ailment. Her face was disfigured and full of sores and warts and lumps, but she was also filthy, and the dirt on her face made it hard to distinguish what was an ailment or what was just plain dirt. Her hair was covered with her shawl, but what was visible of it was matted. What teeth she had left in her head were broken and black, and as she approached them, her breath caused them to turn away from her.

'Do you have the leprosy?' asked Alice. 'I have seen this before in a man, and he looked just like you,' she said.

'All I know is that I am cursed with this, but in a way it is my blessing. So far, it has kept all at bay and allowed me to live in peace. There are so many poor souls on these hills that are persecuted by one evil or another.' Pointing straight at Alice, she said, 'I have a gift of foresight, and I know who you are and how you have come to be here. I had a vision about you. I know the reason for your journey and the precious stones that you have in your other world.' She laughed.

Turning towards Seth, she said, 'and you, my poor friend, you have been caught up in this web of darkness. You are the innocent one. All you seek is to return to your own time and to be rid of the spell that holds you forever in its grasp. I know you both seek the help of the great wizard. I am probably the only person on the whole of this vast moor who knows where he is.' She laughed loudly, knowing she held the advantage over them.

That night, Alice offered to cook some of the meat and vegetables and to boil some herbs for a hot drink. The woman thanked her and Alice got on with the task. As the night wore on, Seth asked the woman who she was.

'I am known as Eida of the copse. I have lived here all my life, since my father and mother disowned me after I became unclean.'

She told Seth and Alice of the events that had brought so much pain and spilt so much innocent blood. She said that Aldfrid and his followers had first settled there some years ago on the hills.

'They came peacefully as farmers, but then not long ago Arthur came north to raise his army in order to fight Morgana. He had a quarrel with Aldfrid. Arthur does not trust the Saxons; he says they are heathens, and meddlers in dark deeds. He suspects they had come here to create a kingdom of their own, and he could not accept that.'

'Arthur is a powerful man, and Aldfrid and his people decided to take shelter in the caves until he had gone through. Arthur is partly right. Aldfrid does have mystical powers, but only uses them for the good of his people. He will, of course, not hesitate to use them against Bordagan if he threatens harm. However, he knows that Bordagan has great powers of his own and he is wary of making a challenge that could result in peril for his people. So he waits, and hopes that Arthur will return and put paid to Bordagan and his men.'

'How did Bordagan come to be here on the moor, and when did he come here?' asked Alice.

'Bordagan arrived a few days after Arthur had moved north. His mission is to find Merlin and hold him to ransom against Arthur.

'Arthur is now growing older, and the years of fighting with Morgana have wearied him. He decided he would raise an army big enough to drive Morgana away once and for all. He has been travelling for two months now, all the way up country and along the borders of Wales, avoiding the Picts and the Druids. They are others whom Arthur has little time for. He has made his way through the central lands to the north, and has recruited men all along the way.

'He intends to amass them all on his way back south. It was his intention to go as far as Carlisle before making his way back, but for some reason he has stayed with the monks on the hills above Parbold for the past two weeks. One of his knights told me that he draws inspiration from them.

'Merlin, too, is a man of some mystery, but he is also a man of peace. He decided not to travel further north with Arthur. He hides somewhere in the caves on these hills. Morgana knows this, and although she too is trying to rally an army to match that of Arthur, she sent her general, the butcher they call Bordagan, to hunt down Merlin. She believes that, if she has Merlin, Arthur will be weakened.

'So far, Merlin has managed to evade capture, but that is no thanks to Bordagan. It is through the kindness of the people who have lived on these hills since the beginning of time.' Eida suddenly stopped talking and cocked her head to one side as if listening for something. She began to look very afraid again.

Then, with one almighty crash, the door of the cottage was smashed into a hundred pieces as four men burst in, swords in hand.

The old woman shrank back against the wall and hissed at them. One of the men held a torch high, and as the light exposed her face, they recoiled in shock. Then, in came another, who seemed to be in charge. He told the men to take Alice and Seth and get out. Once they were outside, he told his men to burn the building to the ground with the old woman inside.

Alice protested, but Seth stopped her, indicating to her that there was nothing to be gained by this. Alice reluctantly became silent. The four men tied their hands and dragged them off. As they were leaving, they could see that the building was well alight, and the sound of wood crackling was so loud. They listened and looked for signs of the woman. They could not hear any sounds of anyone screaming or calling for help. They could only hope that the old woman had some secret way out of her cottage.

All that night they were dragged along, uphill and down dale. They walked for ages and had no idea where they were. Before daylight came, they reached a large camp. They were taken to a tent. Inside the tent there were stakes, driven deep into the ground, to which there were men and women shackled. Some looked as if they had been beaten. They all looked hungry and cold.

The guards secured Alice and Seth to two of the stakes, and left. After a while, daylight began to filter through the tent. Two guards entered, and unfastened two of the women and took them out. The two women returned, carrying bowls of bread and jugs of water. They went round to each of the prisoners and gave them bread and a drink.

As one of the women reached Alice, she looked at her and asked where she was from. She could tell by Alice's dress that she was not one of them.

'From a land and a time far from here,' was all Alice said. The woman looked unsure and didn't seem to trust Alice.

'Fear not, woman; I would not be in chains if I were your enemy,' said Alice.

This appeared to put the woman at some ease, and she smiled slightly.

'We will talk later,' said Alice. As the woman made her way along the line, she continued to give water to the other poor unfortunates, looking back at Alice from time to time. When everyone had been fed and watered, the guards shackled the two women back to their posts and left the tent. Soon there were whispered words going around. Seth said he suspected it was they who were the topic of conversation.

During the morning, two others were brought in and chained up next to Alice and Seth. Seth made conversation with the new prisoners, and attempted to find out as much as he could about where on the moor they were and if anyone had any knowledge of the old woman they had met the day before.

Two men who were tied across from Seth and Alice assured them not to worry too much about the woman known as Eida. They said she had some unique ways of surviving, and they were sure she would be around somewhere on the hills. Seth was pleased to hear this news. He said he hoped the man was right.

'If we can get free, that old woman is our best chance of finding Merlin, but we have to find her first, providing she is still alive'.

'You'll not find Merlin; nobody knows of his whereabouts. He is keeping his head down and well away from Bordagan,' said the man.

A woman who was shackled close to Seth told him that Eida was suspected of being a sorceress, and that Bordagan had heard of her magic. She said Eida had lived on the moors longer than anyone she knew. She was thought to be a hundred years old, and had ways of escaping from the clutches of the likes of Bordagan, or anyone, else, for that matter.

Seth explained about being dragged away and watching the cottage burning. The woman smiled.

'It will take more than a few flames from Bordagan's men to rid these hills of Eida. Many have tried before him and failed, and no doubt others will come and try, too.'

It was clear in the light of the day that this was Bordagan's main camp. There were a lot of armed men and horses all around.

Some were practising their fighting skills, while others were in the process of making weapons. It was a formidable sight to see so many men armed and ready for battle. Seth tried to guess how many men there were in the camp, but with them all running around and doing so many different things and going in opposite directions, it was impossible to tell. He estimated that there could be as many as two hundred or more.

There was no sign of Bordagan, and Seth

suggested to Alice that he was away somewhere with more of his men. It seemed unlikely that he would attempt to take on Arthur with only two hundred men; there had to be others, and they were probably with Bordagan, somewhere out on the hills.

'What is it you want with the wizard anyway?' asked one man. Seth hesitated, and thought carefully about his answer.

'We have come from a land and a time far away from here, and we don't know how to return to our own place. We have need of his knowledge of how to return.'

'Aye, and where would this land be?' asked the man.

'Far away, in a great forest and in another time,' replied Alice.

This didn't satisfy the man. He was about to ask more questions when a loud cry and cheering went up outside the tent. Drums banged and horns blew.

'Bordagan!' said one, with alarm in his voice. Others cowered and curled up, pretending to sleep. There was excitement and renewed life in the camp. Many more voices and the sound of horses indicated a large gathering of men.

'I'd keep your mouth shut about Merlin if you want to see the morrow,' whispered the man who had been talking to Seth.

After a while, the tent entrance burst open and in came six men. They unfastened Alice and Seth and dragged them from the tent. Whispering and muttering from the other prisoners brought a loud shout from one of the guards, telling them to 'Be quiet.' Silence was instant. They all knew a beating was coming, should they disobey.

The tent they had been held in was on the outskirts of the camp. As they were led away, in the light of day, it was clear to see just how large this camp was. The two of them were dragged through the rows of tents, and past men who looked evil beyond belief. They were taken into the centre of the camp, where there stood a huge central tent. This had to be Bordagan's quarters.

Poles were at every corner, and single black pennants with the symbol of a skull flew from each of them. On reaching the tent, the party stopped and one guard entered the tent. He emerged after a moment and waved them forward, into the tent. Inside, there was another inner tent. The covers were pulled back, and they all entered the main part.

Along the sides of the quarters were seats, with shields and lances adorning the walls behind. At the far end there was a large bed covered in wolf-fur blankets. And at its side, sitting upon a large wooden throne-like chair, was Bordagan himself. He was a big man, his size enhanced by the clothes he wore and the fur he had draped around his shoulders. Leaning against the arm of his seat was his sword. His hand never left the solid gold handle, his fingers stroking it, as if he longed to bring it into action.

'So, Master Seth, we meet again.' Bordagan recognised Seth right away from their previous meetings, albeit from another time, hundreds of years apart.

'My lord Bordagan.' Seth bowed his head in acknowledgement. 'I do not know how I have come to be here, my lord, I …' Bordagan raised his hand, stopping Seth from saying anything more.

'You are here because I willed it, and I willed it because of the company with which you travel.' Seth looked at Alice, and she returned his look and raised her eyebrows.

Alice knew there and then that she was the quarry that Bordagan sought, but why? Bordagan looked straight at her and beckoned her to step forward.

'I know of your mission and of the precious stones that you carry—or should I say 'carried'— with you before you arrived here in my time. Now you seek to find the wizard Merlin in the hope that he will get you back to your time and allow you to continue with your duty, and deliver your precious runes." Bordagan spoke his words with a smug look that left Alice and Seth in no doubt that he was in full control of the situation.

'So, if you know all this and you are so powerful, why do you not just take whatever it is you want and have done with it all?' said Alice. She spoke with a confidence and an air of dissent that sent gasps and mutterings around the room from Bordagan's men and from Seth. No one spoke to Bordagan in that tone. No one had ever questioned his power or authority before.

Bordagan's look changed; first it was one of anger, and then he smiled and laughed. 'If it were not for the purpose I have in mind for you, you would be on the end of this blade by now,' he said.

'I have no doubt you will put me to that blade once I have served your purpose,' said Alice. Her manner amused Bordagan; he was almost beginning to like her arrogance.

Seth looked around at the faces of some of Bordagan's most trusted men. They didn't seem to understand what was happening here anymore than he did.

'I wish to be alone with the woman,' said Bordagan, waving his arm, indicating to everyone to leave. Two men stepped forward and took hold of Seth, dragging him out of the tent.

'Are you sure my lord?' asked one of the men, concerned for the safety of his master. Bordagan assured him everything was all right and that he just wanted to talk privately with Alice Bond.

Once everyone had left and the curtains had been drawn, Bordagan stood up, and walked across the tent to where the seats were. He invited Alice to join him and to sit beside him.

'The stones you were carrying are of no consequence to this particular time or to me, because as yet they do not exist. But you are a woman who has spirit, and you have powers not unlike my own. The difference is, I am known as the evil one around here, and you are the innocent.'

'Go on,' said Alice.

'We are both different, but we both want the same thing. We both want to find the wizard they call Merlin. Here is my offer to you. You stand a better chance of finding the wizard, because the people of these hills do not have reason to mistrust you, whereas I am hated. If you find him and tell me of his whereabouts, I will allow you to go back to your time and fulfil your mission in peace.'

'And if I refuse?' asked Alice.

'If you refuse, you will not see your time again.

Remember, it was I who brought you here in the first place. Cross me and the only thing you will see is the blade of my sword as it enters your heart.' Bordagan smiled intimidatingly.

'How can I trust you?'

'Madam, you have my word as a fellow warlock,' he replied, the smirk still on his face. 'Think about it if you need to, but do not keep me waiting too long.' Bordagan clapped his hands and the guards re-entered.

'See that this woman and her companion have good food and a comfortable place to rest,' he ordered.

The guards allowed Alice to walk freely from the tent. She turned at the entrance and nodded her head towards Bordagan as a gesture of thanks.

Outside the tent, Seth was waiting, still shackled. One of the guards untied him and escorted them to a smaller tent. Once inside, they were brought water to wash with, hot salted meat and vegetables and fine wine. The food was very welcome. Seth was anxious to know what Bordagan had wanted with Alice. When she told him, his first thought was, 'What a wonderful idea', but Alice wasn't so sure.

'Bordagan thinks the people of these hills trust us, but we both know that isn't so. You remember Aldfrid's words and how Will Strong cast us out. Not everyone trusts us; word will have spread, and it is not going to be easy for us to gain the trust of these folks,' said Alice.

'If, as the old woman in the prison tent says, Eida is still alive, then we must try to find her and gain her help and her trust. She says she knows where

Merlin is.' Alice nodded her agreement with what Seth had said.

'Do you really think we can trust Bordagan's word?' asked Seth. Alice shook her head. She wondered if there was any other choice, but she wasn't anyone's fool and she wouldn't be rushed into making up her mind.

They sat and ate their meal and drank the wine, and discussed what to do. They decided that there was nothing for it but to agree to Bordagan's proposal and hope that he would keep his word.

After they had finished, they called the guard and asked to speak with Bordagan. The guard went away, returning a moment later and asking them to follow him to his master's tent.

'You have reached your decision?' asked Bordagan.

'You give us your word that we will not come to any harm if we agree to your 'wishes?' asked Alice.

Bordagan gave his word, then in the same breath he laughed, and said, 'You have my word, but you do not really have a choice, do you?' Then he laughed even louder before summoning his guards to take them away. They could still hear him laughing as the guards escorted them away. Instead of taking them to the small tent where they had spent the morning, the guards took them to the tent where the other prisoners were being held.

They were tied again to the posts again, and told they would be taken back to the moor after dark.

'That's so you won't find your way back here to cause mischief to Bordagan,' said the woman who had earlier told them about Eida.

'It wouldn't be difficult to find this place, but why on earth would we want to come back here?' replied Seth.

'How come he's letting you go? You must be some use to him, or are you taking his side?' The woman had a look of mistrust on her face.

Alice was quick to get in first before Seth made up some unbelievable tale.

'He thinks that we may be able to lead him to Merlin. He knows he has no hope of finding the wizard himself, and he feels we may know where he is, or that we have friends upon the moor who can lead us to him,' said Alice. She felt it better to tell the truth rather than create suspicion among people who had a hatred for Bordagan.

'And what has he promised you in return for this treachery?'

'He has assured us of free passage back to our home if we help him.'

'Ha! And you really believe him?' said the woman, chuckling.

'Keep your voices down,' said Seth. 'Whatever happens, we will stand a much better chance away from here. We will just have to take our chances and see where it leads us.'

'If you're not careful, you will have enemies in every camp, and sure as Arthur is King, someone will have your heads on a stake,' said one of the men sitting close by.

'My advice to you is that you must make up your mind whose side you are on, but remember, there are three forces to be reckoned with. These moors are a very dangerous place for everyone right now, and it will soon get worse,' said the old woman.

'How can it get any worse than it already is?' asked Alice.

'You will learn, and that is why it is best that you choose who your friends and who your enemies are quickly.'

Alice wondered what the woman meant by this, but it was clear she was not going to say anymore. They obviously didn't trust her and Seth, and probably with good reason. Who would, considering Bordagan was just going to let them go? Even though Alice had told them the truth, it was hard to gain the trust of these people.

'What will happen to you, and why you are here in the first place?' asked Alice.

'We are here because we are all from the same settlements that Harold and Aldfrid are from. That was, until Bordagan came onto the moor and scattered everyone. He is holding us ransom in the hope that Aldfrid and Harold won't make trouble for him. Bordagan's business is watching what Arthur is doing for his mistress Morgana. He also thinks if he can find Merlin and do away with him, then Arthur will be much weakened.'

'What will Aldfrid decide to do?' asked Seth.

'Nothing. He will bide his time, as he knows that if he tries to free us, Bordagan will not hesitate to kill us all. But Aldfrid is more worried that Harold will make the situation worse. He is out for revenge for having his settlement burned to the ground. Aldfrid has tried to rein him in, but Harold is his own man. We are lucky that he only has a few men; far too few to wage an attack on a camp of this size.'

It was clear from the woman's voice that she feared Harold's foolishness.

Chapter 8

Making Peace With Aldfrid

Late that afternoon, as darkness fell, the guards came for Seth and Alice. But before they entered the tent, the old woman again warned them to choose well who they wanted for their friends, and asked them, if they saw Harold, to tell him of their fate. Alice promised she would. The guards came in. They unshackled the two of them, then blindfolded them before leading them away.

The weather had turned even colder, and there was a feeling of fine snow mixed in with the wind as they walked. It was howling a gale, and the snow was stinging their faces they walked. They kept their heads down for protection.

After they had been walking for quite a while, the guards stopped, untied them and removed the blindfolds. This was a welcome relief, as at least now they were able to hold their capes more securely over their faces, giving some much needed cover from the bitter weather. The wolf-fur wraps that had been given to them by Will Strong helped to keep out the wind.

They walked for hours before the guards told them that would be as far as they would go with them. Alice looked at the one who was the leader, and asked where they were.

He laughed. 'You're on the moor, you stupid woman. Now the rest is up to you.'

Alice glowered at him, as she did not like being

called stupid, and took note of the man's face. As the guards walked away, the anger was still with her, and it stayed with her even when they reached the top of the hill. Alice raised her staff, pointing it towards him and muttered some words that Seth didn't understand.

The guard suddenly tripped and fell down the side of the hill, tumbling head over heels, falling and falling for a hundred yards or more. Two of the other guards scurried down the side of the hill to help him. Alice smiled.

'Was that your doing?' asked Seth, who was also laughing.

Alice just turned. 'Come on,' she said. 'We need to find some shelter from this wind.' Neither of them recognised any part of the moor. It was a case of wandering until they found somewhere to rest.

As they walked, Seth made it clear to Alice that his distrust of Bordagan was growing by the hour.

'That man is worse than evil itself. You must not hold faith with his promises; he will not help us. Once he has what he wants, I fear he will discard us like a wasted piece of bone from his table.'

'Do you think I am a fool, Seth? I listened to what was said by those poor wretches back there, and as far as I can see, we are alone in our quest to find Merlin, and if we do find him, we must, above all things, protect him if we are to have any hope of gaining his trust and his help.'

As daylight slowly broke, Seth thought he recognised where they were. He could see far down the valley, and in the distance was the ruin of Eida's bothy. The guards had brought them back to the same place they had been taken from. Seth made in that direction, with Alice following close by.

As they got nearer, it became obvious that if Eida had been trapped inside the building, she would have had no chance of surviving. All that was left of the ramshackle building were the two large wooden upright posts that supported the roof, and even those were badly charred. The stone hearth and fireplace were still there, but everything else was completely destroyed.

Behind the old bothy there was the copse, and running along the edge of that there was a small but very healthy row of hawthorn bushes that backed onto the section of the house which had collapsed before the fire. This was the part where Eida had been hiding when they first found her. Even that part of the building had burned away to nothing.

Surrounding the bothy was a small wall, and above that, an embankment leading up onto the moors edge, which would give some protection. Seth suggested they should shelter behind the wall and light a fire to keep warm. They had walked for hours before the guards set them free, and both of them were in need of some sleep.

But first, Seth walked into what was left of Eida's bothy, looking for any signs of her or her body, but there was nothing. No bones or ashes. Alice said that could be a good thing, and that Eida may have escaped the inferno and could still be alive. They gathered wood from Eida's stockpile to burn—at least that had survived the bothy fire. They lit a fire and began to settle down, pulling their fur pelts tightly over them.

They slept soundly for what seemed like hours. Then Alice woke to the sound of more wood being put on the fire. She rubbed her eyes and assumed it must be Seth, but she was wrong.

'Eida!' gasped Alice. 'You're alive and well.'

The sound of Alice's excitement woke Seth, and he too couldn't believe his eyes.

'How in God's name did you get out of there alive?' he asked, pointing at what was left of the bothy.

'It will take more than a few flames from Bordagan to see me off.' Said Eida, then she hushed them and told them not to trust the safety of this place.

'You are being watched by Bordagan's men all the time. They cannot see you as long as you stay down by this banking, but if you move away from there, they will see you. They are high up on yonder hill and are watching to see what your next move will be. They know you are here because of the smoke from your fire,' she said.

Seth stood up and looked upwards towards the hill; he could just make out a few puffs of smoke from what must had to be their camp-fire, but he couldn't see any people.

'Trust me, they're there,' Eida assured them.

Eida asked them how they had come to be free from the butcher's clutches. Seth explained about their meeting with Bordagan and what he had said to them. Alice also told Eida about the other twenty or so prisoners that were being held by Bordagan. Eida nodded, and said he would be using them to trap Harold and bargain with their lives for his surrender.

'What are you going to do about his request? Are you going to go along with what he asks?' asked Eida.

Seth and Alice both shook their heads and assured her that they had no trust in his word that he would help them.

'I have had dealings with Bordagan before, and I know of his treachery,' said Seth 'We will use him as he is using us, and hope that we can use his plans to our ends, but also to damage him.'

'And how will that work?' asked Eida.

'I haven't worked that out yet, but I will,' said Seth, smiling.

Then he asked her what she had meant the last time they spoke about the people of the moor being the only ones Merlin trusted. 'Who are these people, and what is the position with them and Aldfrid?'

Eida said they were mainly Celts and some Saxons who had been there long before Aldfrid had arrived from the north east. Aldfrid befriended them, and they trusted him.

'Some of them are Harold's people. They are the ones that Bordgan holds prisoner,' said Eida.

'The first thing we must do is find Harold and see if he will meet with Aldfrid. We must find a way of freeing those people,' suggested Alice.

Eida shook her head. 'I believe I can trust you. My senses tell me you will not betray the people of these moors, but before you do anything foolish, I must warn you—Arthur has heard about Merlin's troubles and is said to be preparing to come back to the moors to confront Bordagan. There will be a huge battle when Arthur returns.'

Alice wondered if that was what the old woman in the tent at Bordagan's camp had been talking about when she said the situation was going to get worse.

'Surely that is even more reason to free the prisoners? If Arthur attacks, Bordagan, will he not use those poor souls as a shield?' asked Seth.

Eida assured Seth and Alice that Harold and Aldfrid both knew the position and were trying to find a way to get them free, but the timing would have to be just right.

'There is no chance of a straightforward fight between Aldfrid and Bordagan. Bordagan is far too strong for that,' warned Eida.

Eida sat behind the banking, out of sight of Bordagan's spies, and told them of her lucky escape from the fire. Behind the boards were Seth and Alice had found her hiding the first time they met. Eida told them there was a tunnel behind the boards where they had found her hiding the first time they met, that went the length of the hawthorn hedge. Eida had managed to get down the tunnel before the flames had engulfed the bothy.

The tunnel was still there. It had been crudely dug in a hurry some years earlier by some friends of Eida. There had been work done on it since, and it sufficed Eida's needs. It had saved Eida on more than one occasion. It was a good place to store food. From under her cape she produced some cold meat and cheese. This was indeed a welcome sight to the hungry pair.

Eida suggested they stay where they were until after dark. They had slept for the biggest part of that day, and it would soon be going dark again. They agreed, and Seth decided to collect some more wood. Luckily, Eida's bothy had had a good store of wood for her fire. This had been kept away from the main building, so it hadn't gone up in smoke when Bordagan's men burned her house to the ground.

As he went to gather the wood, Seth looked up towards the hill where Bordagan's men were. He could see the smoke from their fire, but there was no sign of them. He knew they would be lying on the cold grass, watching them somewhere. He did all he could to stop himself from waving to them.

When darkness had fallen, Eida suggested they let the fire die down so the light would not give much away. Bordagn's men would assume they were asleep, and hopefully relax their guard. She wanted to sneak them away and down into the hidden tunnel.

'We will hide in the tunnel until the fire goes out. The guards will see there is no movement and will come down to investigate. When they see you have gone, they will leave … Mind you, I doubt they will go back to Bordagan with the news that they have lost you,' She said, laughing, 'not if they value their lives. We can then go and take shelter in the caves where Aldfrid and his men are.'

'I don't think that is wise. Aldfrid has said he doesn't trust me. He thinks I am evil,' said Alice. He said he'd had a vision about me.'

'He will listen to me, said Eida. He knows me, and I will tell him of my visions. All will be well, and anyway, what other options are there with all that is happening?'

That night, as the fire died down, they crept to the

back of the ruined bothy. Eida pulled back a bush, exposing the entrance to the tunnel beneath. The three of them climbed down, the hole and into the tunnel. Seth was the last one down and then Eida pulled the bush back, covering the entrance. They crawled along for a few yards, then settled down and waited until morning.

Sure enough, as daybreak came, they heard the guards above. Panic was in their voices as they realised Seth and Alice had disappeared. After a short while, all went quiet and they were gone.

Eida slowly pushed the bush out of the way, crept out of the tunnel and looked around to make sure they really had gone. There was no sign of anyone anywhere. Alice whispered to Seth that she had concerns about going back to Aldfrid. He had expressed his mistrust of her in no uncertain terms the last time they had met. She feared that if Eida couldn't convince him that they were to be trusted, their lives could be in more danger than from Bordagan. She suggested they try to find Merlin without help from Aldfrid or Bordagan.

Eida returned to the tunnel. 'I know of your fears and I understand, but you must believe me. What I say, I say with confidence. Aldfrid will not harm you; he will believe me and trust my judgment.'

'Why do you want to help us so much? We have done nothing to gain favour from you, and you don't know us. Why do you trust us?' Alice's voice had a tone of some mistrust of its own.

'I told you, I have visions that come to me, and I had such a vision of you. I know you are lost souls here on this moor. You are caught up in something over which you have no control. But the mission you are taking in your own time is one of good. Although, you are an undesirable in your own time, you were the best person to undertake your mission,' said Eida, pointing straight at Alice Bond.

'I too am in a similar situation, here in my time. People have great mistrust of me. Some of that is because of my being unclean, but also because of my visions and powers. Aldfrid knows me, and he is wary of me, but he knows I will only use the powers I have for the good of the moor and those who wish me no harm. Fear not, for Aldfrid will not harm you,' said Eida.

Seth looked at Alice and nodded his approval. She reluctantly agreed, and they made their way from the tunnel. After walking for no more than a few minutes, they arrived at the top of a deep and quite wide gorge. Using their staffs to steady them, they slowly made their way down the side of the hill. At the bottom, there was a beck that was full and flowing with some power. Eida led them along the side of the beck to a stone bridge, which they crossed.

Once they got over the bridge, there was a narrow muddy path winding its way up the other side of the gorge. Eida led the three of them up the path for a short way, after which it flattened out onto a wide space. There was a much wider path leading down from the upper reaches of the moor. Alice wondered where this led to. In front of them there was a large flat slab of rock, rather like a wall. Gorse covered all the surrounding sides of the rock.

Alice thought they had stopped just to get back

their breath and that they would then be making their way upwards along the larger path, but Eida waved them over to the huge rock.

She pulled away some of the gorse bush, exposing an entrance. The three of them squeezed past the thorny bush and into a passageway. Once inside, they were surprised to see how light it was. Stones in the roof and the walls of the passage shone brightly, lighting up the whole space.

In front of them was a staircase that had been cut out of the rock. Eida explained that this had been there for hundreds of years. No one knew who was responsible for building it, it was so old. She summoned them to follow her down, and they did. They walked for some time. Every passage they went along was lit the same way, with the bright stones shining from the rock.

Eida stopped, and told Seth and Alice that they were nearing the main cavern. She said it would be best if they waited there until she had spoken to Aldfrid. They did as she suggested. Alice was relieved that Eida would be the one to break the news to Aldfrid of their return to his caves.

They sat down as Eida made her way along the passage. There was no noise of men or any kind of activity, which Alice thought strange, and said as much to Seth. He just shrugged and told her not to worry.

Alice asked how many days they had been in this time slip. Seth said he'd lost count, but thought it was at least five. These were disheartening words to Alice. She had only been given four days to deliver her package to Squire Hoghton. She suddenly felt very low. It was as if all was lost, and there was no more reason to care about getting off this vast moor and away from the tangled situation she had found herself embroiled in.

Now it didn't seem to matter what Aldfrid's decision was. Nothing could repair the harm done or replace the time that had been lost. Seth tried to assure her that they would get back to their own time soon, but his words made no difference.

Then there was the sound of people coming from the direction of where Eida had gone. The sound got louder, and from around the corner, they saw Eida and half a dozen of Aldfrid's men. With them was Will Strong. He smiled as he saw them.

'Welcome! Eida has explained your presence here on this moor to Aldfrid, and also of the visions she has had of you. She has assured us of your loyalty to our cause, and we trust her judgement ... Welcome!' He held out his hand to Seth, who took it.

'Aldfrid wishes to speak with you. He needs to know what the situation is with the prisoners that Bordagan is holding. I told him the terms under which Bordagan released you, and that you hold no faith with the word of that butcher,' said Eida.

The party made its way to the main cavern. It took some time to reach there. They followed one tunnel and then another and another, twisting and turning in different directions. It was no wonder they couldn't hear any sounds of people. The maze of tunnels was enough to block out any noise.

As soon as they arrived in the main cavern, they were led straight to Aldfrid's quarters. When they entered, Aldfrid stood to greet them.

'Eida has spoken to me of her visions and her knowledge of you both, and especially the journey you have taken. Please forgive me for my earlier mistrust of you. I knew there was something strange about you, and I cannot take any chances,' he said, 'but Eida is the wise one of these hills and has never been wrong before in her judgements. I need you to tell me what you know of Bordagan's camp and the whereabouts of my people. Do you know where in the camp are they being held?'

Food and drink were brought into the chamber, and Alice and Seth told Aldfrid everything they could about being led to Bordagan's camp, and the tent where the prisoners were being held. They told him how many men they estimated Bordgan had, but said they could not be sure of the numbers because men kept coming and going all the time.

Aldfrid thanked them for this, and told his guards to make up comfortable beds for his guests and to see that they wanted for nothing. The guards bowed and left the chamber.

'Tomorrow, I will meet with the elders and we will decide what action to take. Arthur is aware of Bordagan and what his purpose is on these hills; we hear he is making ready to return soon. Although Arthur is no friend of ours, he is preferable to Bordagan. I have sent word to Arthur that we are prepared to fight alongside him to rid this evil from our hills. I am awaiting his reply.' Aldfrid shook hands with Seth and with Alice.

The guards showed them out of Aldfrid's chamber and to the quarters they had prepared for them. Eida picked up her cloak and her staff and made her way towards the passage that led away from the cavern.

'Where are you going?' called Alice.

'I am returning to my own place. This is not where I belong. I would not be comfortable here, and nor would these good folks be comfortable having old Eida around them. It is best I make my way back. Our paths will cross again soon, you can be sure of that.' She waved, and walked off down the passageway. Alice wondered how anyone could possibly live in that draughty, damp tunnel cut out of the ground.

Chapter 9

Battle Plans Are Made

It was two days' march away from the great moor, and Arthur's men were busy, making ready to leave and head back to confront Bordagan. Arthur had been fortunate enough to raise a reasonable army, but he doubted it would be large enough to take on Bordagan. His intention had been to travel on for another week, and hopefully enlist more men for his fight against Morgana, but the news of Bordagan's mischief had caused him to change his plans.

Arthur had already managed to rally others on his travels north, and he was to collect them on the way back. He now had with him a force of around four hundred, although half of them were nothing more than mere farmers and crofters who had struggled to make a living from the harsh lands of south-western Northumbria. They'd considered it better to fight in the service of the King than to fight the land.

A further one hundred of them were long bowmen, loaned to Arthur by local elders and landowners of some standing. These men were dedicated and swore allegiance to the King. Others were made up from descendants of Romans who had stayed on after the legions had left—sons and grandsons of Romans who had married locals and who had now become farmers. They were strong men, and eager to serve.

Everyone was doing their bit, getting ready to march off. It would be a hard two days ahead of them. Carts were being loaded, weapons prepared and food cooked, ready to serve to the men as they needed it.

As all this was going on, few noticed the rider gallop into camp, but he was expected and was met by two of Arthur's knights as his horse came to a stop. A soldier took the horse, leading it away to be fed and watered. The rider shook hands with the two knights, and then he was taken to Arthur's tent. He was not one of Arthur's own men, but one of Aldfrid's.

Inside the tent, he approached the table where Arthur was sitting He bowed, and waited for Arthur's response.

'Who are you, and what news do you bring me?' asked the King.

'Sire, I am Hubert of Great Hill, and I come with news from my lord Aldfrid. He fears your attack on Bordagan will endanger the lives of many of our people who are being held prisoner by the butcher. Aldfrid is certain Bordagan will use those poor souls as a shield, and he asks for time and some consideration, so that he can devise a plan to free our people before you engage him.'

'I see … This is indeed a troubling situation. Does Aldfrid have a plan to release his people?'

'He does, my lord, but it will need stealth and cunning, and perfect timing. He also places his men at your service, sire; we are about a hundred and twenty in number, and although we are not all fighting men, we will, in the very least, cause some mayhem and distraction to Bordagan.'

'This is welcome news. Tell Aldfrid to make

ready. We must keep in close contact and plan this carefully so your people come to no harm. How long will it take you to return on horseback?'

'No more than a half a day, my lord.'

Arthur was pleased to hear that Aldfrid was prepared to wage war with him against Bordagan. They could put their differences to one side this time. Bordagan was the force of evil and if it meant siding with Aldfrid—a Saxon—or the greater good, then that was the way it had to be. After all, Arthur wished to have no claim to these moors or to anything of Aldfrid's.

Arthur thanked Hubert for bringing his news, and the knights escorted him from the tent. He was given food and a drink and was soon on his way. As he rode from Arthur's camp, he had a feeling that all was going to be well. Arthur had appeared to be a good man. A man of great integrity: He looked around Arthur's camp; it was clear to him this was a well organised force. Bordagan was in for the fight of his life. The only problem was, although Aldfrid knew where Bordagan's camp was, he had no idea how big it was or how many men he had.

Hubert rode back to the moor, and met no resistance from any of Bordagan's men. As he approached a point where he could enter the caves, he dismounted and looked around before leading his horse inside. The entrance was covered by boards that were covered with turf to make it look as if it was part of the hillside.

Hubert told Aldfrid what Arthur had said. He suggested it may be a good idea to ride, and meet with Arthur in person in order to show him solidarity.

Aldfrid said he would consider doing that. He agreed that it was important to be seen to be sincere in their quest to rid the moor of Bordagan. It was Aldfrid's duty to protect his people, just as much as it was Arthur's to save his friend and confidant, Merlin.

That night, Aldfrid sat with his most trusted men and discussed what Hubert had told him. He decided he would ride to meet Arthur. During the discussion, a guard entered Aldfrid's chamber and told him that Alice wished to speak with him. He summoned her in.

'Sire, you remember the first time we met you, and we showed you the trickery that had been inflicted upon my companion Seth? Sire, why not allow Seth and myself to go to Bordagan's camp. We could go in the guise of others like Dregs and infiltrate them. We might be able to learn the whereabouts of your people and what may be the safest way to free them. We could also learn more of the strength of Bordagan's army.'

Aldfrid thought for a minute. 'There may not be enough time. Things are moving quickly now, and …'

'Sire, forgive me, but we could leave now, before nightfall, and be at Bordagan's camp before daybreak. We could be back here by the noon tomorrow. Two hours should be enough to learn all we need to know. We could also prepare your people in readiness for what is to come,' said Alice.

'Have you discussed this with your companion?' asked Aldfrid.

'Yes, sire, and he is in favour. We want to help. It is in our interest, if we are to secure a way of returning to our own time.' Alice waited for the King's decision.

'Give me a few moments to think about this, and I will let you know of my decision in due course.'

Alice went back to Seth and told him of her conversation with Aldfrid. It seemed like an age had passed before the guard came and told them to make ready to go. Will Strong came and spoke to them before they went. He warned them that they must not betray Aldfrid and his people to Bordagan, even if they were caught and tortured. Alice and Seth both gave their word that they would rather die first than cooperate with Bordagan. They were led out of the caves by a guide who knew the location of Bordagan's camp. He was to go with them for part of the way, and off they went.

Meanwhile, in Arthur's camp, preparations were still underway as men dismantled tents and loaded them onto carts. Arthur's tent would be the last to be taken down. Large catapults had been built, and were being tested in readiness for confronting Bordagan's forces.

Hubert rode back into Arthur's camp to bring the news that Aldfrid would like to meet with him before the battle. Arthur agreed, and said he would delay moving off until he had met with Aldfrid. He told Hubert to tell Aldfrid he would wait for another day.

Hubert also told the King everything about Alice Bond and Seth. Arthur listened, and raised his eyebrows at such a far-fetched tale. He couldn't believe that people could come from a time in the future, and stated that these two must not be trusted.

Arthur had no time for witchcraft and sorcery. He told Hubert not to discuss those two or their trickery with him again. He also said he would not be responsible for their safety once the battle was over. This unsettled Hubert. Alice and Seth had become quite popular with some of those in Aldfrid's camp. He thought it best to let Aldfrid resolve the matter, and he said no more about it.

Word spread around Arthur's camp that they would be staying for one more night. Tents were hurriedly re-erected and horses were bedded down again. No one asked why; it wasn't considered prudent to question the King's reasons. He knew best, and that was that.

As dusk fell near Bordagan's camp, the rain began to fall, heavy and unrelenting. This would, however, help Alice and Seth. Bordagan's guards would have their heads down under their cloaks, and those who were lucky enough to have tents would not be venturing out in this weather.

They waited, hiding in a shallow cleft of land about a hundred yards from the edge of camp. Torches and fires were the only light, and they decided to try to avoid the main part of the camp that was lit. Sneaking around the back of the tents, they made their way to where the prisoners were being held. Their guide stayed hiding in the cleft, waiting for their return.

It was time to put their plan into action. Seth concentrated, then started to squirm and writhe. He became bent and deformed as he turned from being Seth into Dregs.

Alice, however, did no such thing, but did bend so

as to stoop like an old woman. They silently slipped under the wall of the tent, looking for any signs of guards inside, but all was still.

Quietly, they made their way over to where the man and woman were tied up. The ones they had met the last time were there. Almost everyone was sleeping, except for two new prisoners. They tried to ask who Alice and Seth were and why they weren't tethered like the rest of them.

'Hush! All will be explained soon,' said Alice quietly as she and Seth—or Dregs, as he now was—settled down next to the woman.

Alice shook the woman gently. She looked up at Alice and then at Dregs, and gasped.

'Who are you? What do you want here?' she asked, looking at Dregs.

Alice removed the cape from her face and told her not to worry and that it was a disguise.

'Soon you will all be freed, but we need you to be ready, and you must not give any signs to Bordagan or his men of what is going to happen. Do you have any idea how many men Bordagan has with him here? It is very important; you must think!'

By now, most of the tent had woken. Alice told them all to be silent. The woman's husband said he had been taken on a working party, cleaning where the horses were tethered. He and the others had counted fifty horses and at least four hundred men, but he said there were many others out on the moor who constantly came and went, so there were possibly forty or fifty more horses, and maybe as many foot soldiers.

'So, there are five or six hundred men, and one

hundred horses,' Said Alice.

Suddenly, there was noise outside the tent. 'Guards!' someone said. Everyone lay down, pretending to be asleep. Alice and Dregs lay down by one of the huge poles the prisoners were tied to, and didn't move. The guard entered and held his torch high, looking around for signs of movement. No one stirred. The figure of an old woman and a scruffy, deformed little man didn't seem out of place with the others in there. He grunted and left the tent, satisfied all was well.

After a few minutes, Alice sat up and told the prisoners to be ready. She assured them they would know when the time had come. Then, as quietly as they had arrived, they left by the same way. It was still raining, but not as hard. They sneaked back along the back of the rows of tents. The only sound was of drunken laughter coming from the far side of the camp.

Once back with their guide, they made their way down the hillside and towards the safety of the caves. They bypassed the burnt-out cottage that was once Eida's home. There was no time to lose, events were moving fast now, they had to get back to speak with Aldfrid before he left to meet with Arthur.

They arrived back in the early hours of the morning and were taken straight to Aldfrid's chamber. He hadn't been awake long and was preparing to leave.

'Well, what news?' asked Aldfrid. He wanted to be able to offer Arthur as much as he could to give him a better chance to prepare.

'Bordagan has around six hundred men and one hundred horses. They are well armed, and all are experienced fighting men. We have told the prisoners to be prepared when the time comes.'

Aldfrid frowned at the news of so many men. 'If Arthur has four hundred men, some of whom are no more than farmers, and we have only a hundred of the same, this is going to be difficult at best and near impossible at worst,' he said.

Aldfrid knew he needed to find more men. He immediately sent out messengers to all villages and settlements, calling for all men who were fit to fight to make ready and to arm themselves with whatever they could use as a weapon for fighting. He instructed his messengers to tell the people to prepare beacons on the tops of the highest hills, and that when the time came for the first beacon to be lit, that they should light theirs as a signal. On seeing this, they all had to make their way and gather at Round Loaf Hill.

Two hours before daybreak, Aldfrid and six of his most trusted men left for Arthur's camp. Riding by his side were Will Strong and Hubert. The journey led them down off the moor and across to the hills of Blackrod, and from there they made their way overland to Parbold Hill, above the township of Ormskirk, where King Arthur waited to meet this man who until now had been his adversary.

At the same time that Aldfrid left the caves, men were hurrying in every direction to spread the word that Aldfrid and Arthur were to unite to rid the moor of Bordagan. They were given warning of the great battle that was to take place, and men were rallied to fight.

As Aldfrid and his men got close, Arthur's

men rode out to meet them and escort them back to camp. A fanfare of horns sounded, and beating drums heralded Aldfrid's arrival at the camp of King Arthur. Aldfrid was not used to being treated with such importance, but accepted the welcome graciously.

As Aldfrid's horse trotted the last few feet towards Arthur's tent, the great man himself came out to meet his visitor. Aldfrid dismounted, and both of them gave the polite salute of the arm across the chest. They were not unlike one another in appearance; Arthur was slightly shorter and a little leaner than Aldfrid, but other than that there was very little in it. Arthur welcomed Aldfrid and invited him into his tent. He and Arthur went inside alone, leaving the others to take refreshment elsewhere, away from the private meeting between the two rival kings.

Ale and cold meat were prepared and laid out. The men from both sides sat and warmly exchanged stories as they ate. The meeting was very formal, but friendly. Both men accepted their differences and pledged to put them aside for the good of the task in front of them.

Aldfrid told Arthur of Alice and Seth's visit to Bordagan's camp during the night and what they had found out. Arthur's mood changed; he had told Hubert that he wanted to have no dealings with Alice or Seth. He was quick to inform Aldfrid the same.

'You know only too well of my stance on witchcraft and sorcery. I will have no party with those who profit by such evil. If we are to work together, then these two must not be any part of our arrangement,' said Arthur.

Aldfrid thought this strange considering the reputation Merlin had with matters of wizardry. He couldn't understand the difference, but he said nothing. Obviously, Arthur trusted Merlin, and whatever his reasons were, this had nothing to do with the matters in hand.

Aldfrid assured Arthur that the mission Seth and Alice had undertaken had happened before he had been told of his feelings about them. 'I know how you feel. I too had reservations about these strangers, but I have come to trust them, and they risked their lives going into Bordagan's camp to gather the information we needed. But I will ensure they are kept well away from you, if that is what you prefer.'

Arthur nodded, and said it had to be that way if they are to work together.

The two men sat for over two hours, discussing plans to engage Bordagan. Arthur told Aldfrid he had had many a skirmish with the man before. His hatred for Bordagan was born out of his evil and the sorcery he had used to try to bring down Camelot.

'Morgana idolises the man. In her eyes he can do no wrong. I have tried to put paid to him and his vile tricks so many times in the past, but he somehow survives, whatever the odds against him,' said Arthur.

Aldfrid wanted to tell him about Seth's experiences with him in the past, but held back for fear of antagonising Arthur further. Aldfrid told Arthur that he had sent men all over the moors to try to raise more men for the fight. He said he and his men would be ready when the time came.

Arthur believed it would take him two days to march to the moor. The heavy catapults were needed, and would slow him down. Aldfrid gave Arthur a drawing of the moor indicating where Bordagan was camped. It was on the top of a hill across the valley from Pike Hill, where Harold's settlement had been until Bordagan had burnt it to the ground, taking many of his people prisoners.

'And what of this Harold? Does he join us in this fight?' asked Arthur.

'Yes indeed, my lord, he is ready. He has no more than a dozen men, but every one of them is well armed, and they will fight like lions to free their people.'

'Good!' replied Arthur. 'We break camp this morning and will begin making our way to your moor. We will take up position on Pike Hill, across from the hill where Bordagan waits. My plan is to draw Bordagan into the valley, and then justice and revenge will be Harold's as his Pike Hill fights back,' said Arthur.

Arthur's words stirred Aldfrid, who now understood what people meant when they spoke so well of this legendary king. Both men realised they would be outnumbered by Bordagan. His men were well-armed fighting men, unlike those of Arthur and Aldfrid, who only had a couple of hundred true soldiers. The rest were made up of peasants, and although they were as keen as mustard to fight in the name of Arthur, they were no match for Bordagan's army.

One thing Arthur had on his side was that he

was a man of strategy. He was a former general, and one who knew how to find an opposing army's weaknesses. This battle would test all his strengths and resolve, but if he was to save his friend Merlin, and at the same time free the innocent people of the moor, then that was how it had to be.

By the end of their meeting, the two men had formed an alliance. The only thing they could not agree on was the matter of Alice and Seth. Aldfrid had grown to trust them and wanted to help them, but Arthur would not even hear their names mentioned.

As the two kings walked from the tent, they looked up towards the sky. The rain had stopped and there were breaks in the clouds as the late autumn sunshine broke through.

'I wish you a safe journey back,' said Arthur, 'and the next time we meet, I hope it will be as we run Bordagan from your lands.' This time, the two men embraced. There was a bond and an understanding. It clearly pleased the men from both sides as they waited for their master's instructions.

Aldfrid's instructions were to ride for home, while Arthur's were to break camp and prepare for battle. Loud cheers went up and there was a clapping of hands as Aldfrid and his men rode out of Arthur's camp. A wave of excitement swept through the people. Everyone had the feeling that something memorable was about to happen, but what they didn't know was that the odds were heavily stacked against them.

Riding back to the moor in the light of day was much easier, but it was also far more dangerous. Bordagan's men roamed the moor, constantly looking for signs of Merlin or anyone who might have knowledge of the wizard's whereabouts. For any man who caught Aldfrid, the reward would be worthy of a king's ransom.

Each man was aware of the danger and everyone kept looking in every direction the whole way back, but they were lucky; there was no sign of any of Bordagan's men. As they got closer to the hills, they could see some of their own men returning after delivering their messages to the outlying settlements. Each one of them returned with good news and messages of support. The elders from all the settlements gave assurances that they would be ready. Wood was being collected for the beacons, and swords and spears were being sharpened too.

Aldfrid called a full council of his men and told them of his meeting with Arthur. Then he sent for Seth and Alice and told them of the uncompromising situation that Arthur had put him in with regard to them.

'But the man doesn't even know us,' said Seth. Alice, however, wasn't in the least surprised. She had encountered this from all quarters—from her neighbours in her own time, and now here. It made her wonder how people could form opinions about her without ever having met her. It even amused her, in a way.

'If Arthur doesn't know us, then he won't know whether we are part of your fighting force or not, so I do not see a problem,' said Alice, offering a wry look to Aldfrid.

Aldfrid shrugged, and a thin smile came across his face. 'I am sure we will find some role for you to play in all this.'

As plans were being discussed by Aldfrid and his most trusted men, Seth and Alice rested and talked between themselves. They were still no wiser as to the whereabouts of Merlin, and had no idea how they were to find their way back to their own time. It bothered Alice that if Arthur hated them so much, he might not allow Merlin to help them, and they would be stuck in this time slip forever. Seth tried to reassure her that it would not be the case.

'Do you not think it would be better for us to seek out Eida instead of joining the fight? After all, what good are we, one man and a woman? We would not be missed, and if Eida knows the whereabouts of Merlin, surely it would be better to find him than to wait upon Arthur's mercy,' suggested Alice.

'You may be right. I will speak with Will in the morning and see what he thinks.'

That night, everyone rested. They knew they would need all their strength in the coming days. There was little noise to disturb the peace of the night, apart from the odd snoring and someone telling that person to be quiet.

Chapter 10

The Journey to Pike Hill

Arthur and his army of four hundred had struck camp and had loaded everything onto carts and mules. Oxen were to be used to pull the heavy wooden catapults and crossbows. It was these items of heavy artillery that would slow the journey, but Arthur knew Bordagan had none of these tools of war, and he knew they would help to redress the balance of power.

He hoped Bordagan had no knowledge that he had them, either. If Bordagan knew he had such equipment, he might risk an early attack, and that would take away Arthur's advantage, maybe even finish him. He decided to travel through the night and all through the following day, and then to rest, preferably in a large wood somewhere. There, it would be easier to hide the catapults and crossbows from any spies that Bordagan might have lurking around.

As far as Arthur and Aldfrid knew, Bordagan had no idea of their plans to attack him, and they wanted to keep it that way for as long as they could. Arthur sent out his own spies to look for movement from Bordagan's men. He knew he was reasonably safe for that night and day ahead, but by the end of that time he would only be within half a day's riding distance from the moor.

He was taking a long way round to the great moor. The land was flatter this way, and they felt it would be easier to move the equipment. The last day of the trek would be the hardest. By then, they would reach the point where they would begin the long climb up the hills that led onto the moor. It was Arthur's plan to set up his camp on Pike Hill. From there, he would be able to see Bordagan's camp.

He also knew that by the time they reached that point, Bordagan would be under no illusion of what his intentions were, but by then it wouldn't matter.

Moving in daylight was much easier than at night. And by nightfall, the enormity of the struggle ahead of them was soon apparent. There was to be no use of torches to light the way, for fear of attracting unwanted attention, and the moon was well hidden behind the rain-laden clouds. The ground was already sodden, and the freshly falling rain was soon causing more problems.

The heavy equipment was getting bogged down in certain places. One cart had lost its wheel and had to be unloaded before the wheel could be replaced. This held everyone up. The track at this point was single-file, and there was hardly room for a mule to pass, let alone another cart.

Arthur's men went ahead and chopped branches from trees, and laid them like a mat across parts of the track where it was muddiest. This helped, but the going was very slow. By morning, they only covered half the distance they had hoped to have covered. The men were shattered with having to push and pull the heavy carts, catapults and crossbows, but their resolve was still strong as ever, and they pressed on.

By mid-morning, the rain had stopped and there

were breaks in the clouds. Occasionally the sun shone through, lifting everyone's spirits. But then there was more concern. A brook that Arthur had crossed on his way to Parbold was now a swollen torrent, and in full flow due to the amount of rain that had fallen. Arthur called on some of his recruits, who were familiar with the workings of the land. They began chopping trees down, and then hooked up the heavy horses and calmly led them through the shallowest part of the river.

They began to drag the big trees one after another and lined them up until there was width enough to pull a cart across. They lashed the trees together and drove heavy stakes into the soft bed of the river to stop the trees from moving.

Others were busy cutting smaller branches and were laying those flat across the top of the main tree trunks. With seven huge treesall lashed together and secured, they slowly began to move the heavy carts and other equipment across. The countrymen had done a good job. Not one cart or man was lost in the crossing.

But this had taken up the biggest part of the day, and Arthur now knew he was not going to arrive at Pike Hill as early as he had predicted. He decided to send a rider to let Aldfrid know of the change of plan. It was almost night-time by now. The day had been far harder that he had imagined it would be. The land had changed dramatically in the four weeks since he had come this way. The northern weather had been most unforgiving.

He gave the order to make camp, and allowed fires to be lit behind screens made of tent cloth. It was unlikely that Bordagan or any of his men would venture this far from the moor, and the screens and the woodland in between them and the moor would provide ample cover.

That morning, Seth went to speak with Will Strong about the conversation he and Alice had had the night before. Will was sure Aldfrid would agree to their suggestion, and said he would speak to him about it.

All that day, Aldfrid's men were in a state of nervous excitement. This was obvious from their raised voices and comments of bravado, and the tales of what they would do to Bordagan when they caught him. Aldfrid listened to the comments with a cautious satisfaction, knowing that his men were ready for the fight that lay ahead of them.

That evening, one of Aldfrid's men escorted Arthur's messenger into the main cavern. He told him of the problems they had had that day and how they were a good half day behind with their planned arrival at Pike Hill.

The man was given some light refreshment before being asked to take a message back to his king. The message was to tell Arthur just to arrive there safely and refreshed enough for the fight that lay ahead. Aldfrid told him it was better to be two days late and fit than on time and on their knees. He told the messenger to assure King Arthur that he and his men would be ready and waiting for his signal when the time came. He also informed him that their numbers had since doubled.

He wished the rider well and a safe journey back to his king. The lookout took him back to the cave entrance and watched as he rode off. The rider rode south, away from the area where Bordagan was. It would take him no more than two hours to reach Arthur's camp, and although it was dark, at least it was a fine night and the sky was clear, with a full moon to light the way for him.

After Arthur's messenger had gone, Aldfrid sent for Alice and Seth. He asked them to sit down, and began to speak to them.

'Will has told me what you have asked. I agree; it might be the lesser of two follies if you try to find your own way to Merlin. But once the battle begins, you will have to act with haste, for once it is over, Arthur will come for Merlin and he will be gone.'

Aldfrid was in a relaxed mood, and asked them to tell him about the time from which they had come.

'I was unsure about you both when you came here. We may be pagans, but that does not mean we condone witchcraft and sorcery, and yet you do not appear to be evil people. You have offered to help us, and that shows there is good in you,' he said.

Seth explained how he was just an ordinary man who had been travelling through the wood when he was met by the one they called the Gatekeeper. He explained how the Gatekeeper had been bewitched by Bordagan many years before this time. He said that the spirit of Bordagan passed through time, wreaking misery on anyone who he crossed such as The Gatekeeper, and now he appeared to trap people who were passing through the great wood, and used them for his own evil end.

Alice then told Aldfrid about the stones and said that she had two of them in her possession before meeting with the Gatekeeper. She said she was now unsure what to do about them, and whether it might be better to give them to the Gatekeeper and allow him to rid himself of the curse of Bordagan, or deliver them to the person she was meant to take them to.

'My suggestion to you is, if you are fortunate enough to meet with Merlin, ask him what you should do,' said Aldfrid. 'What does history tell you of the great battle that lies ahead between Bordagan and us?' He waited with some apprehension as to what Seth and Alice would tell him. They looked at one another and both shook their heads.

'Sire, there is no mention of this battle. I have heard nothing of it at all,' said Seth. Alice agreed with Seth. 'I have heard nothing either.' This worried Aldfrid. Did it mean there was some annihilation of one side or the other, and it was so bad that no one dared speak of it?

'Maybe it is a sign that the battle won't take place. Perhaps Bordagan will flee,' said Aldfrid.

'Sire there is one thing that our history suggests to me,' said Alice.

'Go on.'

'If the story of Merlin's stones is true—and I have held two of them in my hand—then Merlin must surely survive, because the legend says that he leaves the moors in peace.

The stones are said to be a gift for all the kindness shown to him by the people of the moor. There was said to be one stone that was then broken into five pieces. The stones were then cast far and wide. It is said that whoever finds all five pieces and places them together will find the entrance to Merlin's cave. Once inside, they will find items that will bestow great powers upon them.' This reassured Aldfrid.

By the end of their conversation, Aldfrid was under no illusion as to the full extent of the evil that Bordagan was capable of. What he could not understand was how Bordagan was still causing problems many years hence. There had to be some great mysterious force at play. Could it be that these stones held the answer?

'I suggest you rest tonight, and then you can set off before daybreak to find Eida. Tell her of the battle plans, and that you have my blessing for her to lead you to Merlin. Make sure she understands the urgency of the situation, and tell her to be careful. There is no room for error or mischief.'

Seth and Alice knew that Aldfrid meant Eida should not play tricks with Bordagan. For all her ailments and deformities, she had a wicked sense of humour, and she knew how to use it. Aldfrid wished them good fortune, and said he hoped he would be victorious and would see them after he and Arthur had chased Bordagan from the moors for good. Alice and Seth returned his good wishes and left to get some rest.

Chapter 11

Merlin

It was still dark when they set off to Eida's secret tunnel. It wasn't far, and as they approached, they quietly called out Eida's name. After a moment, she emerged, peeping out from the far end of the tunnel near the ruin of her bothy.

The three of them went down inside the tunnel, and Seth told Eida everything that was about to happen in the days ahead. He also told her that Aldfrid had given his blessing for her to take them to Merlin. She laughed.

'It is true! I do know the whereabouts of the great wizard. It is I who see that he is given the food offered to him by the others of this moor. He trusts only me, but that does not mean he will speak with you or anyone else, even if I ask him to,' she said.

'But you will ask him for us, won't you? You must tell him of the position we are in, and how urgent our situation is. We must return to our own time, and I need to ask him about the stones. I need to know what is the best thing to do with them.' Alice was almost pleading with Eida.

Eida said she would speak to him, but warned them not to build their hopes up. She set off almost straight away, before daylight arrived. All Seth and Alice could do was wait. They didn't have long to wait before Eida was back.

'What is the matter? Why are you back so quickly?' aked Alice.

179

'I have seen him. Fear not—he's not far from here. He says he has had visions of you and the worry you carry with you. He will see you, but makes no promises. We must leave right away. He wishes to hear of Arthur and Aldfrid's plans. He is very concerned for Arthur's safety.' Eida picked up her staff and summoned the pair of them to follow her.

'Keep your eyes open for Bordagan's men,' she warned.

Leaving the tunnel, the three of them made their way upwards, away from the ruined bothy in the direction of where Bordagan's guards had been watching them only two nights before. They reached a single track that weaved its way around the side of the hill before climbing up again and then disappearing.

Now they were on grass and heather, and once around the other side of the hill, they began to walk down until they came to a large mass of gorse bushes. Eida led them to the far side of a big gorse bush, and using her staff, she banged on a rock that was sticking out of the ground.

The gorse bush moved away from the hillside slightly, exposing the entrance to a cave. Eida went inside and bid Alice and Seth to follow her. Once they were inside, she pulled the bush back across the entrance to the cave. The first part of the cave passage was as black as night, then a flicker of light appeared from the left. They made their way towards it. Eida clearly knew her way. Soon the light was much brighter, and eventually they arrived in a large cavern. At the far end of the cavern was a rock.

'I have brought them to speak with you, Merlin,' said Eida quietly.

Out from behind the rock stepped the man that was Merlin, the great wizard. He didn't look very spectacular, thought Alice. He had long white hair and a beard to match. He was a man quite diminutive in stature, and yet there was an aura about him that told her he was special.

'Please, come forward that I may see you,' he asked.

Seth and Alice stepped forward. Eida stayed in the background. Merlin offered them a seat as he pointed towards a makeshift bench by the side of the cavern wall. All three of them sat, and Seth was the first to speak.

'We are not from this time. We have been bewitched in some way and caught up in a strange time slip. All we want is to return to our own time,' he said. Then Alice reminded him of the other problems that were even stranger.

'My friend here seems to forget how he came to be here, and that it is not the first time Bordagan has used his magic to bring him here to this time. Bordagan knows of your special stones, two of which I was in possession of. He has asked us to lead him to you, but all we want to do is return to our own time, and I need to know what to do with the stones.' Merlin raised his hand. 'First things first. These stones you speak of? I find it most peculiar that you are here and speaking of something that has not even occurred yet, but there is possibly a twist to all this, and maybe all will become clear soon. But first, tell me of Arthur and Aldfrid,and what is to be done,' said Merlin.

Alice decided to let Seth tell Merlin about the battle that was going to take place. Then Eida interrupted. 'Do not forget the poor souls who are prisoners of the evil butcher, and who will probably be the first to perish at his hand once he knows of Arthur and Aldfrid's plot.'

Merlin nodded. 'All in good time. We will have to see how they are to be saved before the battle commences, and we will,' he said. He asked how long it would be before the battle lines would be drawn. Seth said Bordagan would know of Arthur's intentions by noon tomorrow. It was then that Arthur and his army would arrive at Pike Hill.

'Then we must act before daybreak tomorrow,' said Merlin.

He then wanted to know how Alice and Seth thought he could help them, as he knew nothing of time slips. Alice said she could only imagine that the stones played some part in this strange scenario.

'I know that you have certain magical powers of your own, and my instincts tell me that these will help us when the time comes.' Looking at Alice, he continued, 'I also feel that you may have been misunderstood in your use of your magic, but I know from my own experiences that Arthur will not tolerate any kind of sorcery.' He smiled. 'It is amazing how I have got away with the things I have for thus long. Arthur is a good man, but his mind is narrow in such matters.'

Merlin stood, and the rest of them did the same. It was clear that their audience with the great man was at an end for now.

'We will speak again before daybreak tomorrow. I will have a plan and some answers for you by then.'

'But what are we to do about finding our way back to our own time? Can you help us?' asked Seth

'I will study your situation and see what can be done, don't worry about that for now. The most important thing is what lies ahead in the coming days.' Merlin nodded his head slowly in a reassuring way.

Alice stared at him, and a feeling of calm washed over her. She knew that all would be well. Seth and Alice followed Eida out of the cave. Merlin came with them to the entrance and bid them farewell.

It was now daylight. The morning was kinder, calm, dry and sunny, much improved on the past few days. It would be better for Arthur and his men as they made their way overland towards the great moor and onto Pike Hill.

Eida, Seth and Alice decided to walk up to the top of the hill. What neither Alice nor Seth knew was that this was indeed the hill they called Great Hill. Once they arrived at the top of the hill, the view was amazing. Eida pointed out Round Loaf across the valley, and in the opposite direction she indicated to where Bordagan had his camp, and told them that Pike Hill was across the valley from there. They could not see any movement, nor make out Bordagan's tents. Eida said it was probably further over the other side of the hill and just out of sight. Pike Hill was not to be seen either.

It felt very poignant, looking out over the calm moorland and yet knowing that in a day or two's time all hell would break loose as battles were fought. The deer grazing amongst the heather and the birds high on the wing gave no feeling other than that peace belonged in this place. There was no sign of any of Bordagan's men, or of Aldfrid's men. It was just like any other day in the countryside.

Eida suggested that they didn't remain out in the open too long. She felt it may be tempting fate. The hills were full of valleys and small clefts in the hillsides, and Bordagan's men could appear from anywhere at any time.

The three of them made their way down, and were soon back on the path that had led them past Merlin's cave and down the valley to Eida's tunnel. All the time they walked, Eida was looking around. It wasn't that she was afraid of Bordagan's men, just the opposite. She enjoyed the cat and mouse game she played with him, but she didn't want anyone to see her or her companions entering the tunnel by the row of hawthorn bushes. This was her last place of refuge.

The inside of the tunnel was tidy and well-constructed. It had been dug out to a decent height, and the walls and roof had been shored up with timbers from the collapsed part of her bothy, before it had been burned to the ground. She told them that some of Will Strong's men had helped her.

'But I thought everyone was afraid of you because of your ailments?' suggested Alice.

'The only ones who are afraid of me are those who I want to be afraid of me. There is nothing that can be caught from me, save for a few unwanted fleas. The warts, lumps and creases in my face are the result of old age, and years of living in squalor,' she said, laughing. Alice and Seth both burst out laughing too.

In a part of Eida's tunnel, there was an alcove that had been dug out of a large rock which ran along one side of the tunnel; Eida used this as her kitchen. Unfortunately, she had not been able to cook in the tunnel for fear of Bordagan and his henchmen seeing smoke, so any cooked food she had had kindly been supplied by Aldfrid's people. Strangely enough, there was a good supply.

Eida explained that this was because the people knew she had been looking after Merlin. She laughed. 'I do not know how much they think one man can eat, but they sometimes leave enough to feed an army.'

Eida set about slicing some of the cold venison and bread. That day, they all ate well. Eida suggested they try to sleep during the afternoon because they would be up the coming night. She later left the tunnel with a bag full of food. Merlin would not go hungry either. When she returned, Seth and Alice were fast asleep. She left them in peace, knowing they would need to be alert for the task that lay ahead later.

In Bordagan's camp, there was some excitement. One of his scouting parties had returned with news of seeing bonfires being assembled on hilltops. He sent his guards to fetch one of the prisoners from the tent where they were being held. The one they brought to him was an elder who was known to have been close to Harold. His name was Stewart.

Bordagan had him dragged before him. The

poor man was frail and in his seventies. His wife had escaped the raid on their settlement and was now safe in the caves with Aldfrid and the others. Bordagan looked at the man with a stare that left him in no doubt that he considered him to be worthless.

'Well, old man, I am going to give you a chance to be reunited with your wife. Tell me, why are your people building beacon fires on the tops of the hills all over the moor? Tell me the truth, and you will go free. Tell me lies, and you will never see your wife or your family again.' Bordagan sat back and waited for the old man's response.

The man shook his head and looked at Bordagan. 'My lord, how can I possibly know what their reason is for that. Perhaps there is a celebration taking place?'

Bordagan looked at him and smiled. 'I tell you what, you go back to your stake in the ground and talk amongst yourselves, and then in a while I will send for you again. If you give me a sensible answer, you will go free. If you do not ...' He stroked the handle of his sword as he looked down at it. The old man knew what he meant.

'Take him away.' The two guards took hold of the man by his arms, and dragged him back to the tent and then secured him to the stake. Everyone wanted to know what Bordagan had needed him for. He told them, but none of them said anything. They all knew that something was going to happen because of what Seth and Alice had said two days earlier.

'You must tell them it is a celebration, a wedding of Aldfrid's daughter to another nobleman; they will believe that. Tell them the fires will be lit to signal

the calling of everyone together for the celebration.'
This was the best reason they could think of, and
they had hoped that Bordagan would accept the
explanation.

A short time later the guards were back. They
untied the old man and dragged him out of the tent.
His feet were hardly touching the floor, due to the
force in which the two guards half lifted and half
pulled the poor man along.

They walked into Bordagan's tent and straight up
to where he was sitting. He was alone apart from the
two guards. They threw the poor soul to the floor in
front of him. Bordagan took hold of his sword and
placed it between his legs with both hands resting
on the handle. He looked down at the frail old man,
who was by now shaking with fear.

'Well, have you learned anything from your time
with your people? Do we know what the beacons
are for? Think well before you answer me, old man.'
He looked at him and tilted his head to the side so as
to request an answer.

'My lord, I have been told that Aldfrid's daughter
is to be married to a nobleman and that the beacons
are to summon everyone to the celebration.' The
old man bowed his head and closed his eyes, not
knowing what to expect.

'A celebration, indeed. And where will this so-
called 'celebration' take place, and when?' asked
Bordagan.

'My lord, you will only know that when
the beacons are lit. None of us are wise to that
information, but we think it will be soon.' Again, the
old man bowed. Bordagan was silent for a moment.

Then he called the guards and told them to take the old man back to his tent. He called his most trusted men to his side and told them what the old man had said. He said that if it was true then they should be on alert. If the people were going to gather in such a manner, it could be the perfect chance for him to get to Aldfrid.

Chapter 12

The Armies Gather

Some miles to the South and west, but well out of sight of Bordagan and his men, Arthur's army of four hundred men and their equipment was making good progress. The weather had been kinder to them and the ground had become firmer now. The streams and becks that they occasionally had to cross were not as swollen as they had been the day before, and could be passed easily.

There had been no more breakages of the carts or any of the other heavy machinery that was being moved. Nor had Arthur's scouts reported any sightings of any of Bordagan's men anywhere. The morale was high, and from time to time, more men had joined the long line of Arthur's fighting force as they passed through settlements along the way.

The King had decided that they would march until it was dark, and then make camp for the first part of the night instead of marching straight to Pike Hill. One of the scouts had found a large wood about four hours away from Pike Hill. He said it was big enough to offer good cover, and from there it would only take one rider an hour to reach Aldfrid. This would give him plenty of time to ready his men. Arthur sent a rider off to Aldfrid's camp right away; he didn't want to wait, and he needed to give Aldfrid as much time to be ready as he could.

The next day was going to be crucial for Arthur to get into a safe position on the hill across from

Bordagan's camp. The moment Bordagan knew that Arthur's army was approaching, he would prepare to attack. Arthur's battle plan had no room for failure. The timing had to be right.

He would rest his men for the first part of the night, and then under cover of darkness, they would move onto Pike Hill. They had to be there and in position before daybreak. Arthur's message to Aldfrid was to have his men near to Bordagan's camp by daybreak, and for them to be ready to attack from the rear when needed.

Arthur's messenger arrived safely at Aldfrid's camp, and a guard escorted him into the caves to speak with Aldfrid. The messenger told Aldfrid of Arthur's progress and of his king's wish that he should be ready. He said he would send a signal when the time was right for Aldfrid to make his move.

Aldfrid thanked the man and then called all his men together. His main worry was the prisoners at Bordagan's camp. If they didn't get them out before the battle began, they would surely be slaughtered. At that point, Harold arrived at the camp of Aldfrid, bringing with him all the men he could muster.

Will Strong suggested they send someone to tell Eida what was about to happen. She had said that she and Seth and Alice would go to the prisoners' tent and free them when the time came. Harold said it should be him and his men doing this deed, but Aldfrid told him that according to Eida, Merlin himself was trying to devise a plan to free the prisoners, and if anyone had the power to do this, Merlin could. And in any case, he needed Harold and his well-armed men to fight alongside him when the battle began.

Reluctantly, Harold agreed, and Aldfrid sent one of his men down to Eida's tunnel to tell her of the plans. He also sent messengers to all the settlements on the moor, telling the people there to be ready and watching for the first beacon being lit that coming night.

What Aldfrid didn't know was that the sign of the beacons being lit would draw Bordagan and his men away from his camp. They would think it was the start of the celebrations, and it was Bordagan's plan to send a large raiding party in search of all those attending the celebration. This would be good news for Arthur, because it meant Bordagan's force would be split in two, but it could create huge problems for Aldfrid and his men. They could have a battle of their own on their hands before they could get into position.

As soon as Eida was told of the plans for the battle, she went off to speak with Merlin. Alice and Seth went with her. Again, Eida banged her staff on the rock by the side of the gorse bush and the bush slid away.

Once down inside the cave, they told the wizard what was about to happen. Merlin stared into his fire as the flames danced mesmeizingly.

'I have a feeling of foreboding about all this. The fire is telling me something about the fires you are going to light. This is not good and could place your friends in great danger. You must go and tell your leader to light one fire only, and to light it well away from where he wants his men to be. Bordagan will attack the site of the fire, and that would be perilous for all those there. Tell your leader I have seen this.'

Merlin looked worried, and Eida, Alice and Seth knew they had to do as he asked.

'I will go right away, alone,' said Seth.

Eida asked Merlin if he had thought of a plan to free the prisoners before the battle. Merlin nodded.

'The lighting of the beacon fire will draw away many of the guards. While this is happening, you must sneak into the camp. Take one bowman with you. He must cause another distraction in a part of the camp away from the prisoners. Burning arrows are always a good distraction. This will be your chance to free the prisoners,' he said. 'If the battle is to begin at daybreak, you must act just before then.'

'Will you join us?' asked Alice.

'I will be where I am needed, when I am needed,' Merlin assured her.

Seth arrived at the entrance to Aldfrid's cave and was quickly shown to his chamber. He told him what Merlin had said, and about the vision he'd had. Aldfrid thought for a moment, and then he immediately sent fresh messengers to all the camps.

Next he sent a party of men to the top of Coppice Hill to create a huge bonfire, and told them to wait there for a signal to light it. Coppice Hill was in the opposite direction and out of sight of Round Loaf. The plan was that, as soon as the fire was lit, all the men from each camp were to make their way to Round Loaf. Bordagan's men would then head to the fire at Coppice Hill, but there would be no one there.

By the time Seth returned to Eida's tunnel, the daylight was beginning to fade. Eida said they should hurry and make their way back to speak with Merlin. They collected their fur pelts, some food and their staffs, and followed Eida to meet with Merlin. They were joined along the way by one of Aldfrid's most trusted bowmen. The meeting with Merlin lasted no more than a few moments. Merlin had made up his mind; he wanted to go with them and join the fight, but Aldfrid's man said that was not wise. He pointed out to Merlin that it was too much of a risk. If Bordagan caught him, that would be the end of the fight. Bordagan would have his most prized possession, and if that happened, Arthur would give up.

Merlin realised he was right, and decided to remain in his cave until the battle was over. Before they left, he called Alice to one side.

'If I can't be with you, then I want you to take this,' he said, passing her a long staff of his own. It was made from blackthorn and was anything but straight; it was topped with a carving of a goats head. 'This will protect you and give you strength to stand up to your enemies. Use it wisely, and bring it back to me after you have defeated Bordagan. If you see Arthur, hold the staff high, and he will know that you are a friend of mine.'

Alice wondered about that … after all she had been told of the way Arthur felt about her and Seth. She was hoping they would be well away from any part of the battle. Her job was to free the prisoners and lead them away from Bordagan's camp.

She thanked Merlin as she laid down her own

staff, and as she took hold of Merlin's staff, she immediately felt a strange surge, something she couldn't explain. It went all the way through her body and right to her feet. She looked at Merlin. He just nodded and smiled at her.

'Go now, and be careful,' he said. The four of them thanked Merlin, left the cave and made their way upwards to the top of Great Hill. They stopped when they reached the top, looking around, apart from the whisper of a breeze in the grass, there was no sight or sound of anything stirring.

It was now dark on the hills as they set off across the moor. They decided to head straight across in the direction of the hillside where Bordagan's camp was. There was little light from the moon as they set off. They walked quickly but quietly, listening all the way for the sound of any of Bordagan's men who might be out on the hills, but there was nothing.

It took them less time than it had the last time they paid a visit to the prisoner's tent. They reached the cleft in the ground that was just a short way from the edge of Bordagan's camp. They lay down on the damp ground, covering it with pelts to protect them from the wet, and waited for the signal that would be the lighting of the beacon. They knew it might be a while. From where they lay they could see across the moor to both Coppice Hill and Round Loaf.

Aldfrid had told them that Arthur hoped to move onto Pike Hill after dark, and that the beacon light would be sufficient to distract Bordagan long enough for them to get into position without being seen. Aldfrid said he didn't think the battle would begin before daylight, although it would be obvious to everyone by then what was going to happen.

Aldfrid's bowman said, 'Bordagan will be expecting Arthur to have only a ramshackle army of nothing more than peasants. He doesn't know that Aldfrid will be against him as well and attacking him from another side. I have been told that Arthur has a plan that he hopes will even the odds up, but he hasn't said what that plan is.'

They had discussed what they had to do, and knew it had to be done quickly. As soon as the light appeared they would have to move fast and release the prisoners before Bordagan knew what was going on.

Looking up at the position of the moon, Eida said she thought it must be well after midnight. 'Surely Arthur will be at Pike Hill and getting into position by now,' she said.

The bowman decided he would crawl to the top of the brow to see if he could see or hear anything. He returned a few minutes later and said that all was deathly quiet. There were only a few torches lit and no sign of any movement of men anywhere.

He had hardly settled down when the light of a burning arrow shot across the night's sky. It came a good distance from the left of Pike Hill, but they knew it was Arthur's signal, telling Aldfrid that he was ready.

They were right. Over on Coppice Hill, the beacon was being lit, a huge beacon that Bordagan was bound to see, and hopefully he would take it to be the start of the wedding celebrations. Aldfrid knew that Bordagan's arrogance would not allow him to hold any kind of celebration, and he knew

Bordagan would seize this opportunity to try to capture him, or at least to round up more prisoners in the hope that someone might know Merlin's whereabouts.

A horn sounded in Bordagan's camp.

This was it; the four of them quickly gathered the things they needed and quietly made their way up the brow of the hill. Lying down on the top, they watched as Bordagan's camp came alive. More torches were lit, men were mounting horses and there was an air of excitement.

Aldfrid's bowman was beginning to get angry. He could sense the thirst for blood echoing from the voices of Bordagan's men as they shouted to one another. They knew there was sport to be had that night, and the thought of so many people in one place made it all the more appetising.

The bowman had seen this thirst for blood before. He had escaped by the skin of his teeth on the first night Bordagan came onto the moor. His father had been killed in that attack. His mother was now being cared for in the caves. It was because of what Bordagan had done to the people of his settlement, and in particular his father, that he wanted to come here this night.

Now was the time. They made their way down towards the tents that ran all along the edge of the camp. Because of the excitement that was taking place, all Bordagan's men had gone into the centre of the camp to join in the fun. Only the prisoner tent had anyone left in it.

One guard had stayed by the entrance to the tent. The bowman, who was an excellent shot, took him down with one straight and true arrow. It was so swift a shot that he didn't even make a sound as he fell.

Eida, Alice and Seth all entered the tent, telling the prisoners to be quiet and do as they were told. One by one they were untied and then lined up just by the entrance to the tent. Altogether, there were thirty-one prisoners.

Four of them had been badly tortured and were in a lot of pain. They said the others should leave them and save themselves, but Alice would have none of that, and neither would Eida. The stronger of the men were told to help the injured. They were sent out of the tent first and given a head start.

Outside, the bowman had moved back away from the edge of the camp to a place where he would be able to see if any other guards were coming. He was ready with his bow, and half-hoping that some would come. It had given him some satisfaction, taking down one of Bordagan's men, and yet he craved to even the score further, but none came, much to his disappointment.

Once the injured were over the brow of the hill and out of sight, the others quietly made their way up and away from the camp. They were led down to the cleft where the rescuers had been hiding. No one had thought about what was to happen from here. It might be too dangerous to attempt to head further down the hill towards Eida's tunnel, but if they remained there, Bordagan might easily find them.

Then the bowman had an idea. 'I suggest you all stay here. It will only be a few hours now before Bordagan knows of Arthur's presence on the Pike, and when he does, he will have other things on his agenda. He will not have time to come looking for you, and by then Aldfrid and his men will be here. I will go up to the top of the hill and away from this place, and if I see any of Bordagan's men coming in your direction, I will draw them away from you.' He looked for their approval to his plan.

'Go then, but be careful,' said Seth.

He left, but the rest of the party remained, keeping their heads down and not speaking a word. Seth thought for a moment, and then he took out the tiny bag that held Milo and Fog. Alice looked at him and smiled. She knew what he was about to do. He lifted Fog out of the bag and held him in his hand. The rest of them looked on in amazement at this tiny ball of mist.

Then he took out Milo, and as the little ball of light danced above his hand, he told it to go and keep watch. The light danced some more before shooting off upwards towards the top of the hill. A gasp from some of the people was the only noise, but Alice asked them to hush.

Then Seth looked at Fog. 'Do your business; hide us,' he told it.

Soon, the small ball of mist was covering the whole of the cleft of land where they lay. They were completely hidden beneath the mist. As long as they remained quiet, no one would know they were there.

The bowman had made his way safely to the top of Bordagan's camp, and had moved slightly away from the direction of Seth and Alice and the others. The excitement was still high amongst Bordagan's men. None of them had gone back to their tents, and as yet nobody had found the dead guard or noticed the prisoners were missing, but the bowman knew it wouldn't be long before they did. He was about seventy feet from the tent where the prisoners had been held, and had a good view of anyone approaching.

By now, Bordagan's horsemen had gone. It wasn't clear if Bordagan himself had gone with them on the bloodletting ride across the hills. It would have been better if he had, thought the bowman. That way, he would have to arrive back before an attack on Arthur could be made, and the more time they had to prepare, the better.

Chapter 13

The Battle Begins

The bowman stayed alert, and watched as two men walked towards the tent where the prisoners had been. He and Seth had dragged the dead guard inside the tent before they left. The two men looked around, but there was no sign of the guard. They thought at first that he must have gone to join in with the rest of them.

Then one of them decided to take a look inside the tent. The bowman acted quickly. He loosed his first arrow—again, it was straight and true, and hit the man squarely. He fell to the ground. The other guard heard the thud, and turned to see his companion fall. He lifted his horn from his belt and put it to his mouth, but before he could raise the alarm, the bowman had loosed his second arrow.

Back at the cleft where the prisoners were hiding, Seth sat up. He shook Alice and told her someone was coming. He had his head to the ground, listening. He didn't know if it was Bordagan's men or Aldfrid's. Eida decided she would have a look.

She stood up and walked upwards, out of the misty cleft of land. Just down the shallow valley was Aldfrid with his army—two hundred men armed with whatever they could use. Some had swords and pikes, a few had long bows, while others had come with nothing more than the tools they used on the land. What they lacked in armoury, they made up for in bravery.

They were slowly and quietly making their way towards her. Seeing the figure of this strange woman rise from nowhere out of the mist stopped them in their tracks. Then Will Strong recognised her, and laughed quietly.

It was still dark, but only just. Daylight would soon be with them, and then the fight would begin. Eida walked down to speak with Aldfrid and Will. She suggested they didn't go any further yet, because they were only a short way from the edge of Bordgana's camp. Aldfrid agreed. They would lie low there until Arthur made his move. The grass was deep and had a good covering of bracken all around. This provided good cover for Aldfrid and his men. Eida went back to the cleft and told the others that Aldfrid had arrived. As soon as the battle cry went up, they would move away and back to the safety of the caves. The excitement was building, and nerves were obvious in some, as they could be seen visibly shaking. Alice did her best to calm everyone. Out of the mist and into the centre of the group came Milo, straight over to Seth. The ball of light danced up and down and then shot straight into Seth's pocket, to where the small bag was.

Seth wondered what this action meant, as he had never seen Milo behave like this before. Then he realised that Milo had never seen so many people preparing for a fight before. This must have confused the tiny light, and it had decided it would be best to go back to the safety of the bag.

The sound of a horn, then another and another, resounded all over the hills, and drums began beating too. The noise sent shivers down their spines. Seth and Alice looked at one another and Eida told everyone that it must be the start of the battle.

This was the signal for the escaped prisoners to begin to make their way down the hill and away to the safety of the caves. Eida, Seth and Alice remained. Eida said she was going nowhere; she wanted to see Bordagan get his comeuppance.

Far across the valley, on the top of Pike Hill, a hundred torches and beacons had been lit. The beacons burned damp wood and wet grass, creating smoke to hide what Arthur did not want Bordagan to see, and it was working. Light was just about coming. This was Arthur's way of announcing to Bordagan that he was back and ready to take him on.

Aldfrid sent scouts to the tops of the hills to see what was happening. One of them came back and reported seeing Bordagan's men riding like the wind, back towards his camp from the direction of Coppice Hill. He would know by now that it had all been a ploy to distract him. Guards rushed to the tent where the prisoners had been. They saw the bodies of the guards and ran back to raise the alarm.

The bowman saw them, but did nothing to stop them this time. It would have been folly to try. He kept his head down and watched as the chaos unfolded. There was no sign of Bordagan himself in the camp. The bowman thought he must have been one of the riders that had gone off to Coppice Hill.

The bowman could see that the riders were almost back at the camp. There were so many of them, and true enough, there was Bordagan, riding at the head of them. If only he had been closer; the bowman wished he could have loosed an arrow at the butcher himself, but he was too far away, and there were too many people around him.

Bordagan jumped off his horse and made his way to the top of the hill. He looked out across the valley. He wondering how this army of men could have arrived there without being seen by any of his scouts. After a moment, he made his way back to his tent, followed by his senior knights.

Battle plans were made. Bordagan knew Arthur could not have raised an army of true fighting men in the short time he had been away. He suspected they would be mainly peasants, farmers looking for glory in the name of the great King Arthur. This gave him some satisfaction. His mouth watered at the thought of ripping Arthur's ragtag army to pieces.

'Gentlemen, Arthur has decided to return. I suspect he thinks we will run away. He probably believes his army of farmers will scare us.' The whole tent erupted with laughter.

'I have a plan that will see this over quickly, and the man who brings me Arthur's head will be the richest man in this land.' There was more cheering as Bordagan raised his sword.

Over in Arthur's camp, his men had secured the huge catapults and crossbows in place. He had positioned them well out of sight of Bordagan's men. They would have no idea that Arthur had such armoury at his disposal. In fact, he had no idea of what Arthur did have. Arthur had given his knights instructions on how the battle should be fought.

He had also discussed the plans with Aldfrid, so when the signal came, Aldfrid would know when to launch his attack. All that was needed now was daylight.

Arthur was ready. His men knew exactly what to do and what was expected of them. Bordagan was also readying his men, and had plans of battle of his own. He was convinced it would be a one-sided fight.

He lined his one hundred horsemen up all along the hilltop. They carried lances, and maces and swords which would be used after the initial charge with the lances. Behind them, he had his foot soldiers. The first row of another hundred would charge with pikes, ready to run through anyone who got in their way.

The second row of foot soldiers carried maces and swords as well as shields. They would be used to mop up any remaining stragglers. To each side of Bordagan's main force there were fifty men, armed with bows and crossbows. Bordagan had decided he would keep the remaining men behind with him.

Arthur played along to Bordagan. He knew what he would be thinking, and to some extent he was right. Arthur did not have the same fighting force that his enemy had, and therefore tactics would play a big part in the outcome of the fight.

Arthur positioned himself on his horse with his six most trusted knights flanking him, three to either side of him. He stood proudly and menacingly in front of his row of one hundred horsemen. Then, as if to tease Bordagan, from behind his main force he brought out his army of peasants.

They made their way to the front of Arthur's horsemen. Two hundred of them lined the entire side of Pike Hill, some carrying pikes and swords, and others only armed with sharpened wooden staffs and farming tools.

Bordagan's men howled and whooped at seeing this makeshift bunch take up their positions. His drums beat even louder. His horsemen raised their lances and swords in a threatening manner, shouting all the while.

'This man must be sick with some fever to consider attempting such a battle, but if that is what he wants, let us not disappoint him, men. I will take his head to Morgana myself and then she will be mine,' he said, laughing.

What Bordagan could not see was what Arthur had over the other side of the hill. It was only a few yards down the hillside, but the bushes and the smoke from the beacons provided enough cover.

Arthur's own drums were beating just as loud as Bordagan's, and his knights were waving their pennants and shouting too. As the peasant army lined up, Arthur stirred them to make as much noise as they could. They had to show Bordagan that, although they were far outnumbered, they were not afraid. This they did, and it was not because they were told to, but because they wanted this fight as much as Arthur did. They were proud to be standing alongside Arthur on that hillside on that cold morning in November.

Bordagan and his men waited to see how Arthur wished to commence with this fight. He knew it was not wise to attack upwards towards Arthur's men. It was far better to stage the battle in the basin of the valley below. He also knew that Arthur would see it the same way. He decided to let the brave Arthur make the first move. He didn't have to wait very long.

As soon as daylight was good enough, Arthur looked at his knights and gave the signal to proceed. Horns were sounded, and much shouting and loud beating of drums from both camps signalled the intention to begin.

The command was given, and the peasant army began to make their way slowly down the hillside, banging their weapons against their shields as they marched. They had painted their faces with dyes of all colours and covered their hair with mud. The intention was to make them look bigger, wilder and more fearsome. The wild look became them, and their eagerness for a fight was obvious.

The valley was flanked on both sides by steep hills, with some trees and gorse, but was generally easy to walk over. The opposing armies occupied a hill each. In the bottom of the valley a shallow but quite wide stream flowed. The terrain was good. The land was used for grazing animals. This kept the grass flat, and it would be ideal land for a fight.

As Arthur's men approached the lower reaches of the valley, Bordagan gave the order for his horsemen to advance. At first they moved off in perfect fashion, all in a line and at walking pace. Slowly, the pace gathered and became a trot, and the horses were eager to go, flaring their nostrils and snorting loudly with their heads jolting up and down. Then, as they were near the bottom of the hill, they broke into a gallop. The riders' lances were lowered and the shout to charge was given.

By now, Bordagan's foot soldiers had also set off down the hillside, following at a quick jog behind the horses. They were right behind the horsemen when they reached the lower side of the hill.

At this point a horn was sounded and the peasant army turned and retreated, running back up the hill towards Arthur. Bordagan roared with laughter on seeing this. As his horsemen reached the bottom of Pike Hill, they were riding furiously in pursuit, fully intending to put an end to this ragtag bunch of peasants. Then Arthur raised his sword before lowering it to his side.

The order was given to fire, and a cascade of heavy stones was launched into the air from the catapults, as were huge burning arrows from the massive crossbows. At the same time, Arthur instructed his one hundred bowmen who were also behind the smoking beacons to fire at will.

The shower of stones and arrows rained down on Bordagan's horsemen and foot soldiers. The burning arrows from the huge crossbows crashed into the ground, scattering fire everywhere as they hit the floor. The horses and men were in complete disarray; with the horses rearing up, it took the riders all their time to remain on the saddle.

At least twenty horses and riders were hit by the stones, and other horses had thrown their riders off. The foot soldiers were scattering; many of them had fallen foul of Arthur's bowmen, and many more were wounded. Those who were unharmed were helping the wounded back out of the range of

Arthur's arrows.

Bordagan was fuming; his army were running for their lives. The arrows kept coming and continued to hit those of his men who could not get out of the way fast enough. Virtually half of the first wave of his attack force had been killed or wounded, and his horsemen, who were the pride of his army, had been totally humiliated. The bowmen and crossbowmen that Bordagan had on the sides of the hills had also retreated back to Bordagan's lines.

Back over the hill, behind Bordagan's lines, Aldfrid and his men were waiting for the signal. One of Aldfrid's scouts, who had been watching the events as they happened, reported back and told them of the carnage. It took them all their effort not to let out a huge cheer. But Aldfrid was soon subdued.

'What's the matter, sire? Why do you have such a look of concern?' asked Will Strong.

'I am just wondering what Bordagan's next plan will be. If he knows he cannot attack directly across the valley, where will he go? He will not be beaten by Arthur like that; the man is too proud, and by now he will be too angry. He may decide to retreat and regroup, and if he comes this way, we are no match for his force.' It was clear that Aldfrid was worried and somewhat afraid for his men.

He sent a messenger away and round the side of the hill to Arthur's camp to ask for fresh instructions. The runner was used to such tasks and knew the land well, but he was spotted by one of Bordagan's horsemen, who broke ranks and was soon in hot pursuit. A cry went up from Aldfrid's ranks, though luckily none of Bordagan's men heard the shout, but neither did the runner.

However, Aldfrid's bowman was still on the hillside, hidden in the undergrowth. He stayed down out of sight and managed to shoot an arrow. The horseman was no more than forty feet from him and the arrow struck him cleanly, bringing him down to the ground. Aldfrid's runner carried on, totally unaware of events happening behind him.

Bordagan's men must have seen the rider fall to the ground, but no one else rode out. It would have been certain death for the bowman if he had been seen. He could only assume that his cover had not been seen. In no time at all, the messenger returned.

'Sire, Arthur is redeploying his men and directing his heavy catapults in fresh directions. He does not expect Bordagan to retreat. He believes the man's pride will not allow him to do that. He suspects Bordagan will try to come at him from the sides. He asks that we stand fast and be ready when the time comes.' Aldfrid nodded, and left his men in no doubt that they would wait for Arthur's signal.

Eventually, both armies returned to their battle lines, and although Bordagan had lost a lot of men, either dead or wounded, he still outnumbered Arthur and Aldfrid's combined forces. The only difference now was that his pride had taken a beating. And Arthur still had the surprise of having Aldfrid's men waiting out of sight.

By now, Aldfrid's men were more than ready to enter the battle, and some were getting restless and were saying that Arthur wanted the glory for himself, but Aldfrid knew this wasn't the case and calmed his men, telling them it wouldn't be long before they got their chance to even the score with Bordagan.

At noon, Arthur put the second part of his plan into action. He knew this was going to be a dangerous thing to do, but he needed to break Bordagan's ranks. He doused the fires that had been providing smoke cover. This exposed his catapults and the heavy crossbows.

Arthur sent a runner to Aldfrid, telling him to move his men to the north side of the hill behind Bordagan, and to be ready to support his men on that side. He said he would know when he was needed. Aldfrid told the runner to assure Arthur he would be ready.

He quickly briefed his men and quietly moved them away to the north side. He told Seth, Alice and Eida to stay where they were. Reluctantly, they said they would keep out of the way, but after Aldfrid and his men had left, Eida revealed she had a plan of her own and told Seth and Alice they could either help or stay where they were. Both of them said they wanted to help.

At the same time, Arthur sent thirty of his horsemen, forty bowmen and one hundred of his makeshift peasant army to the north side of Pike Hill. They made a wide sweep of the hill and down into the lower reaches of the valley, but stopped when they reached the stream.

He then lined up the remainder of his horsemen, bowmen and peasants along the top of the hill, directly across from Bordagan. He had spread the catapults and large crossbows and had faced them to the front, and to the left and right sides. If Bordagan did attack, Arthur had every approach covered.

Bordagan had seen Arthur's men move to the north, and thought it odd that he had only sent such a small force.

'I think he is trying to divide us by drawing away half of us and then sending the rest of his men across the valley. But if those are all the men he has, then may his God help him. I will play along with his plan and then attack him from two sides.' He looked at his right-hand man and told him to take fifty horsemen and two hundred men, and go and deal with those who had dared to take him on in the north of the valley.

Bordagan's knight soon had his men organised, and they set off in direction of Arthur's group of men. Bordagan then lined up the rest of his men across the hilltop facing Arthur. His force was still very formidable, even after his losses in the last skirmish. Again, Bordagan held back, waiting for Arthur to make the first move.

This time, Arthur didn't move. He stood firm on his hillside. He knew Bordagan wouldn't risk sending any more of his men into the bottom of the valley to be pounded by the catapults and crossbows. The standoff was tense. Bordagan looked at Arthur and then at the force he had sent into the north of the valley. They just stood there, banging their drums and their shields, making as much noise as they could.

It didn't take long for Bordagan's horsemen and foot soldiers to reach the top of the hill above them. They stood there for a while, outstaring their opponents and banging their own shields. It became a competition of noise for a while.

About a hundred yards behind Bordagan's men were Aldfrid and his two-hundred force of mixed warriors. Most of them were fairly well-armed, but those who didn't have much in the way of weapons made up for that with determination and courage. They too had painted themselves with dyes to create a ferocious appearance.

They were lying down in the deep undergrowth, with just a slight rise and those one hundred yards between them and Bordagan's men, but all Bordagan's men were looking straight down the valley towards where Arthur's men were, and the noise from the drums and the banging of shields was blanking out any sound that Aldfrid's men might have made.

Eida called across to Seth and Alice. 'I have a plan for some mischief that will aid Aldfrid. Are you with me?' she asked.

'What are you plotting?' asked Seth.

Tapping the side of her nose, she said nothing, but began to make her way up the rise towards Bordagan's camp. The rear of the camp was completely empty. Everyone had been called to the front lines, there Bordagan was, or had gone to the north side to take on Arthur's force. It was soon apparent what she had in mind. She crouched down behind one of the empty tents and made fire.

Lighting three torches, she gave one each to Seth and Alice. 'Go, and make mischief.' Then she held her torch to the first tent, setting it on fire. Seth ran one way and Alice the other, setting fire to tent after tent. Eida had the pleasure of being the one to burn the tent that had held the prisoners.

With over thirty tents burning, Eida called to Seth and Alice to make their way back before they were seen. The carnage had taken all but a couple of minutes, and luckily, so far, Bordagan had seen none of it. He had been concentrating on all that was taking place in the north, and at the same time watching for Arthur to make a move.

While all this was happening, Bordagan's knight had given the order to advance down into the valley to take on Arthur's men. This time, Arthur's men didn't retreat; they stood their ground and waited for the enemy to come to them. Aldfrid knew this was it. It was their time to exact some revenge on this butcher who 'had wreaked fire and death on their peaceful hills. He gave them a while to go over the top of the hill and begin their way downwards towards Arthur's men. As soon as he heard the order to Charge, he rose up and gave the same order to his men.

All of a sudden a shout went up from Bordagan's lines as one of his men saw the tent fires raging behind them. Bordagan sent some of his men to deal with the fires before they could spread to the rest of the tents, but it was too late; by now, many of the tents had been totally destroyed and sparks were spreading and starting other fires.

Aldfrid's lone bowman, who had been lying low in the gorse bushes, had witnessed all this, and was taking advantage of the mayhem by occasionally popping up an picking off one or two of Bordagan's men.

As Bordagan's men advanced toward Arthur's force, Arthur's men saw Aldfrid's men come charging over the hill behind them, and then began their own attack. With the joint forces against them, Bordagan's men were completely outnumbered. The bowmen quickly loosed off as many arrows as they could, aiming at the horsemen first. They needed to even the odds up, and they did it very well indeed.

They had almost reached Arthur's lines before they realised Aldfrid's men were closing down on them. As soon as they were close, the bowmen stopped firing and took out their swords. Within seconds, all hell had broken loose as the two sides became intertwined, with swords and maces flailing, man against man and neither offering a quarter.

But Arthur's men and Aldfrid's were too many for Bordagan's, and within no time at all, most were either dead, badly injured or running for their lives. All Bordagan's horsemen had been brought down. His horses had been rounded up, and were now being ridden by both Arthur's and Aldfrid's men. Their now redundant weapons were given to the peasant army, who until now had had only farming tools to fight with. Now the odds were in Arthur's favour.

Bordagan fumed as he saw all this happen. His temper was so vibrant that his horse was becoming restless and almost threw him off. He told his men to stand fast. He would not be beaten. He had to think of a plan, and fast. Following the two skirmishes, Bordagan now only had fifty horsemen and less than four hundred foot soldiers left. He was vastly outnumbered.

Arthur had lost none of his one hundred horsemen and had gained forty more from Bordagan. His force of four hundred had swollen to over six hundred now that Aldfrid had officially joined him.

The two kings sat proudly on horseback on the top of Pike Hill. A Saxon and a Christian side by side. Arthur thought he would never see the day, but he also knew that it wasn't to last. Arthur's faith would not let him be cosseted by a pagan king. As soon as this was over and Merlin was safe, he would leave the hills, but for now the greater enemy was Bordagan, and he had to be stopped. Arthur drew comfort from knowing that once this was over, his and Aldfrid's paths would not cross again.

By now the afternoon was almost done, and the day was becoming much duller. Rain clouds were gathering. Torches were lit along the tops of both hillsides, indicating that enough was enough for one day. Bordagan and his men had chance to lick their wounds and to consider what to do next.

In Arthur's camp, their wounded were treated and all were fed. Aldfrid was given a tent, along with the higher ranked of his men. Later that night Arthur, Aldfrid and their senior knights and men held a meeting.

Arthur suggested that the following morning they should run Bordagan off the moor.

'I propose we split our forces into three. Two forces to each side of the hill, each with fifty horsemen and two hundred men on foot, with a third force of the same leaving before light and making their way behind Bordagan's lines in case he runs.

My thoughts are that he will ride for our camp and try to seize the catapults and crossbows, which we will disable before then, and then if he rides down into the valley, our forces from the north and the south will ride into the valley to take him on and finish the day.' Arthur waited for a response.

'Sire,' said Will Strong, 'what if he does run back onto the moor? will not our force there be outnumbered?'

'Indeed it will, but he will not be expecting them to be there, and the confusion will give us enough time for our men from the north and the south to reach there, our horsemen especially. With luck they should be able to hold him long enough until we are all there,' said Arthur.

Aldfrid agreed the plan sounded good. Then Will Strong spoke again.

'What if he doesn't do anything, and he just stays where he is and decides to fight where he is?'

'More fool him. We would then attack him from all three sides, of course,' said Arthur. His tone was one of disbelief at Will's question. Will could sense the arrogance of Arthur's tone, and left the tent as soon as he could.

'Sire, I would like me and my men to be the ones to leave the camp tonight and be the ones to cover Bordagan's escape. It is, after all, our land that he has violated,' stated Aldfrid.

Arthur agreed, and promised him that until Bordagan was either dead or running from these hills, they would be as one in their quest to rid them of this scourge.

Chapter 14

The Final Fight

With the night now well established, and after everyone had eaten, Aldfrid gathered his men and began to brief them on the plans ahead. Rain had fallen all day, but thankfully it was now dry once again.

Aldfrid's group was made up of fifty horsemen and over two hundred of the men of the moors, who were now far better armed thanks to having the weapons that Bordagan's dead and wounded had no further use for. They had come together over the far side of Pike Hill, away out of sight of Bordagan's camp. They walked their horses in order to keep the noise to a minimum.

Aldfrid told them of the plan that had been agreed. Will Strong grunted at hearing those words. He didn't like Arthur's tone of voice, and had concerns that if Bordagan did turn back toward the moor, then Arthur would leave them to fight him alone. It was no secret that Arthur despised Saxons, and he would never have a better opportunity to kill two birds with one stone.

Will's comments caused some murmuring amongst Aldfrid's men, but he was having none of it.

'This is no time for fighting amongst ourselves. I have spoken long with Arthur. He is a man of great honour, and I trust him. He has told me that we are as one until we have rid Bordagan from these hills.

If you trust me, then you must trust Arthur too,' said Aldfrid.

Will wasn't convinced, but agreed to go along with the plan and, as always, pledge his full support to Aldfrid. When they were almost ready to set off, Arthur came down personally to bid them farewell, wishing them Godspeed.

'By this time tomorrow, you will have your hills back and your people will be able to live in peace again. Bordagan will be either dead or will have fled, and my men and I will never forget the way we fought together with Saxons, against tyranny.'

Because they had to go wide of the moor to avoid being seen by the enemy, it would take them a good four hours to reach where they wanted to be, and some of the terrain was steep and rocky, while other parts were boggy. Aldfrid had thought that if Bordagan was to turn and run, he would head back towards Great Hill and from there make his way to Tockholes Wood beyond.

Aldfrid intended to place his men from the northern side of Great Hill between Bordagan and the wood. From here he would see Bordagan coming from a long way away and would be in a good position to cut him off whichever way he went.

As well as walking the horses, they covered their hooves with sack cloth to quell any noise and to stop them from slipping on the wet ground. They also wrapped all weapons in sacking, too, to prevent any rattling. As they moved, no one spoke a word, and everyone moved as silently as they could so as not to give away their presence.

One man was sent to the cleft where Eida, Seth

and Alice had been watching the events of the past two days. They had to be warned to leave there quickly in case Bordagan did head for the moor and over to Tockholes Wood. They would be surely caught up in his wake. Aldfrid told the runner to tell them to go back to the caves, or at least to Eida's tunnel, and stay there.

Aldfrid and his men took a path away from the moor, heading in the direction of Coppice Hill and then turning left onto the moor itself. This would bring them to the south and east of Great Hill. The hardest part was the climb onto the moor from Coppice Hill. The land here was very hard and was made up of a lot of loose rock. It would be particularly difficult for the horses. Loose stones could cause them to slip, and the noise could carry along the hills to where Bordagan was.

The horses, led by their riders, were treated with exceptional kindness and consideration in the hope that they would remain calm and quiet. Time was taken to find the firmest ground to walk them over, but the hill was so steep that even having the sacking on their hooves didn't offer much help, and some did slip.

It was this part of the journey that took the longest. Once on top of the moor, they found that the land became much friendlier, but they were still quite a long way from where they had to be. The night was cold, but the sky had cleared and the moon lit the moor. In the distance It was possible to see the outline of Great Hill in the distance, rising high into the night sky.

This was a strange situation for the Saxon band of

warriors, because it was in a cave somewhere under this huge hill that Arthur's most trusted friend, Merlin, was hiding, and here they were, protecting a man who was revered by an enemy king.

An hour later they arrived at the bottom of the hill and were on the south eastern side, well away from and out of sight of Bordagan's view. Fires were lit and food was prepared. It was only a short climb to the top of the hill, and that would not be until daylight, although lookouts were posted on the tops. They could faintly see the lights of Bordagan's camp from the top of the hill.

To add to Aldfrid's problems, Eida, Seth and Alice, along with the runner, all arrived at the hill. Eida had sworn she would not run and hide from Bordagan again. It made no difference that she was an old woman, she was as stubborn as a mule. Aldfrid gave up trying to tell her to go away, but warned her not to get in the way.

After they had eaten, the men were told to try and get some sleep. It was still quite a while off until daybreak. Some settled down, but found it very difficult to sleep. The thought and the excitement of what was to come in the following hours was preying on their minds. For some, the morning could not come quickly enough.

While all was quiet and everyone was resting, Eida, Seth and Alice slipped out of the camp and down the hillside to the cave, where Merlin was in hiding. Eida made the usual sounds, and the three of them were soon inside and telling Merlin on what was taking place. Merlin looked worried.

'I have a bad feeling about this. I fear many lives

will be lost before this day is over.' He shook his head slowly and turned away. 'Go now, go to your tunnel and protect yourselves. I must study my runes and find a solution to my fears.'

The three of them left, but instead of going to Eida's tunnel as they had been told, they went back to Aldfrid's camp.

Over on Pike Hill, Arthur's lookouts watched for the first signs of the sun rising over the hills in the east. It had been the same for them. Hardly anyone had managed to sleep that night, and they had no doubt that Bordagan and his men would have had little or no rest also.

At the first sign of the sky becoming lighter, Arthur's lookouts went to tell him that the time had come to prepare. Soon the camp was alive with activity. Horses were being readied for battle and men being given last minute instructions on what was about to take place.

Arthur rode his horse to the top of Pike Hill. Ten of his most trusted men flanked him, five on either side. The drums began to beat, and looking out across the wide valley, Arthur could see Bordagan and his men on the opposite hill. They had heard Arthur's drums calling his men to arms, and had begun their own show of bravado. Their drums were beating too, and pennants were being waved in defiance.

Arthur's men came up from behind Pike Hill. They stood for a while, fifty horsemen on each side of him, and another four hundred men on foot behind them. It was a sight to behold as they all waved swords and pikestaffs in the air.

Bordagan looked on, wondering what Arthur was going to do. He had his archers ready in case they decided to ride straight across the valley at him. He would do what Arthur had done to him on that first day, and rain fire arrows down on him and his men.

But Bordagan was not to get that chance. It soon became clear what Arthur's plans were, as fifty horsemen, followed by two hundred foot soldiers, broke away from the main group and headed towards the south side of the hill. Seconds later, fifty more horsemen, with their two hundred foot soldiers, set off in the opposite direction.

Only Arthur remained on the top of Pike Hill, along with his ten knights. Sitting there on his horse; he looked at Bordagan. The next move was up to him.

Bordagan was no fool; he knew that if he was to ride down the valley to try to attack Arthur, Arthur's men would come at him from all directions. He could try to take one of the flanks out, but he didn't know if there would be any more surprises like there had been the day before.

His men looked to him for answers, but this time, none were forthcoming. The day was lost, so he decided that the sensible thing to do was to head for Tockholes wood and the safety of the cover there.

'Men, the time has come to scatter and make for the great wood beyond the moor. There we can regroup and consider our options. Until we reach there, it is every man for himself.'

He gave the order to burn everything and to set the carts on fire and push them down the side of the hill. It took no more than a few minutes to light the fires. By this time Arthur's men had reached the far sides of the valley. Bordagan told his horsemen to stay with him, while everyone else should flee.

As they turned away towards the moor, Arthur instructed his bowmen to fire burning arrows into the sky. The cloth on the arrows had a special dye that gave off a red smoke when lit. This was Aldfrid's warning that Bordagan was heading his way. Arthur's horsemen saw what was happening and took off in pursuit, but the huge hill in front of them would not be easy to climb, and when they got to the top, they were a long way behind him.

It would be easy to catch and take on the ones on foot, but they knew that Aldfrid would need their help, and it was decided that they should leave the foot soldiers and go after Bordagan.

Aldfrid's men were called into readiness, and his fifty horsemen lined up across the top of Great Hill with the rest of his men spread out behind. Aldfrid had about fifty bowmen, and placed them at the side of the hill with instructions to fire as soon as Bordagan got within range.

Bordagan was well-organised and experienced in battle formations. He saw Aldfrid and his men and knew he had to go straight through them if he was to go over Great Hill. He could not go to the side; the ground there was too soft and his horses would be stuck in the bogs.

He formed his attack in the shape of an arrowhead, with ten men carrying lances at the point. On each side of them he placed a further ten with maces and crossbows, and on the outside another ten with lances. He rode just behind the head of the point, flanked by his two most senior knights. This was a frightening sight for Aldfrid's men. The charge was fast and furious.

Aldfrid looked back over the moor towards Arthur's men. They were riding for all they were worth, but were a good half a mile behind, and Bordagan would be upon them in seconds. He and his men knew it was down to them to stop the man.

As soon as Bordagan's charging horses reached the bottom of Great Hill, his bowmen loosed their arrows. Some struck home, but not enough. Aldfrid's own horsemen lowered their lances and charged towards Bordagan, trying to avoid the point and the lancers. But as they did this, with some success, Bordagan's crossbowmen fired and brought down many of the brave Saxons.

A bolt from one of Bordagan's crossbowmen hit Aldfrid's horse, wounding it and bringing it to the ground. Aldfrid was dazed, but other than that, unhurt. Equally as many of Bordagan's men were killed or injured in the charge, but Bordagan was unscathed. Much to his delight, he saw Aldfrid fall, and turned his horse around.

All around, men were fighting. Aldfrid was on his knees and shaking his head, as if to try to get his bearings. Bordagan smiled and rode towards him. He was going to have his revenge on this Saxon. He drew his mace from his belt and swung it over his head. Aldfrid saw him coming, and managed to grab his shield and hold it above him.

Bordagan smashed the mace down on Aldfrid's wooden shield, shattering it into pieces. He rode on, then turned his horse and came back to finish the job. Again he raised his mace and swung it high over his head, swinging it around and around. Just as he was going to bring it down on Aldfrid, a lightning bolt struck the mace and sent Bordagan crashing from his horse.

Aldfrid looked up. On the top of Great Hill stood Alice. She was holding Merlin's staff high and pointing it in the direction of where Bordagan had been. He knew this was the work of the woman he thought to be a witch or a sorceress. Aldfrid jumped to his feet. Bordagan was about thirty feet from him. He drew his sword and went after Bordagan. He was dazed, and still on his knees.

Aldfrid had to fight his way past battling knights and footsoldiers, in order to reach Bordagan. When he was almost upon him, one of Bordagan's knights rode straight at Aldfrid, knocking him down. Then he rode towards Bordagan and scooped him up on to his horse, and rode off with him in the direction of the great wood.

Seconds later Arthur's men arrived, and the battle was quickly brought to an end. They told Bordagan's men to lay down their arms or die. The foot soldiers were rounded up and told the same. None of them had any fight left in them.

Not long after, Arthur arrived and offered to send some of his men after Bordagan, but Aldfrid said not to. Many men on both sides had died that day. The settlements on the moor would never be the same again, but now Aldfrid had more horses and better weapons, and when the dead had been buried and Arthur had gone, he would deal with Bordagan.

Aldfrid turned, and made his way to the top of

Great Hill. Merlin had arrived and was waiting to greet his king. Arthur walked to him. He held out his hand. Merlin took it and shook it warmly. Alice and Seth were standing alongside the wizard.

'I owe you my life, Merlin. How can I ever thank you?' he asked. He knew the act of magic that had saved him wasn't any doing of Merlin's, but he would never allow himself to be beholden to a witch such as Alice Bond.

'I do not know what you mean. I have done nothing,' replied Merlin with a wry smile. He would not admit to having used such powers in front of his king, knowing how Arthur disapproved of such acts.

Standing behind Merlin were Eida, Seth and Alice. Arthur looked at them and a seething expression appeared on his face. Merlin saw the look

'Sire, I would like you to meet three dear friends, without whom I would surely have starved on these bleak moors during the time you were away,' said Merlin. He hoped this would mellow Arthur, but the King was not bowed.

'Are these the two who are the sorcerer and the witch, who I told you I would have no dealings with?' said Arthur.

Alice stepped forward. 'Sire I am no witch. Many have accused me of being so, but they are wrong, and so are you. My friend here is no sorcerer either. We are victims of Bordagan's evil, and all we ask is to be back where we belong.'

'And where is it that you belong?' asked Arthur. 'Though I personally would place that at the end of a rope,' he spat.

Seth spoke up next. 'Sire, it is true. Bordagan has brought us to this time for his own ends. We come from a time and place far into the future, and all we ask is to be given passage back to our own time.'

This seemed to intrigue Arthur. He looked at Merlin. 'When we have buried the dead and treated the wounded, we will talk of your time in the future,' he said.

Merlin returned to his cave, only this time he didn't seal off its entrance and he allowed anyone who wanted to come inside.

There was calm now on the moor, but there was also a deep sadness. Many good men had lost their lives and others were wounded. All that day was spent caring for the injured and burying the dead. Bordagan's men were made to dig the graves and fetch and carry water to bathe the wounds of those in need. The mood was sombre, but there was also relief in knowing there would be no more bloodshed. The people of the moor emerged from the caves and also helped to bury the dead and dress the wounds of all, including the wounds of Bordagan's men.

Alice and Seth spoke to Merlin about the stones that had played such a big part in their having been caught up in this strange time slip. Merlin smiled.

'It is true. I have been wondering how I can leave a lasting legacy that may protect the people of these hills in the years to come. I have received great kindness from these people while Arthur has been away travelling.

'I know that in one far-off time these people will need my help again. You have all been so kind to me, and I will repay you.' He took his staff and brought its shaft down hard on a stone that was lying on the ground. The stone broke into five triangular pieces.

'This stone is the stone you spake of, and whoever in the future places all five pieces back together again will have the power to overcome any adversity.' Then he picked up the five pieces and walked out of the cave and to the top of Great Hill. He raised his hands and threw the stones high into the air. They spun, and shot off in five separate directions.

'This hill is called Great Hill for good reason, and whoever finds all five pieces of stone and returns them back here will have the powers I speak of. So be it.'

Alice and Seth now knew for certain that the legend of the stones was a true one. Alice knew where two of the pieces were, and either the Gatekeeper or Cedric Hoghton knew where the other three were. What she had to decide was, who was the worthiest of receiving her two precious stones. But first she had to find her way back to her own time.

They all went back inside the cave, and Alice was just about to ask Merlin if he could help them to find their way back to their own time, when in walked Arthur and Aldfrid, along with Will Strong and Eida.

'I have spoken at length with my friends here, in view of all that has been achieved here on these hills in the last few days. But before I give my decision, do you deny that the two of you have powers that are not in keeping with any normal man?' He looked at them, waiting for an answer.

Alice spoke. 'It is true, sire, we are different, but

we come from a time where these powers you speak of are not unusual, and we use them only for good, not evil.' Alice waited for his response.

'Very well, I accept your reasoning. I am happy for you to go in peace to wherever it is you wish,' said Arthur.

Alice looked at Merlin. He nodded. 'I think I know what is needed to return you to your own place and your own time.' He turned to Arthur and the others and asked them to leave him for a while. Arthur gave him a dirty look, turned away and was about to walk out of the cave. He knew Merlin would be weaving some sort of magic, and he did not approve of such things.

Before he left, Arthur told them all to be on top of the hill soon. He had something to say to everyone. Aldfrid looked bemused; he knew nothing of this announcement.

'My Lord, what are you planning?' he asked Arthur.

'It is nothing for you to concern yourself over,' Arthur said, and walked off.

As soon as everyone was on top of the hill, Arthur sat on top of his white stallion and spoke. 'My friends, today has been a great day for good over evil. Sadly, we have lost some good men, but they have not died in vain. Tonight we will celebrate their lives and the peace they have given to these hills. As we speak, my men are preparing a great feast. Tonight we will make merry.' A great cheer rose from the men, but there were still tears being shed by the womenfolk who had lost their men. They were in no mood for merriment.

'Tomorrow, my men and I will leave these hills. We leave you in peace, and may peace remain here for many years to come.' More cheering erupted.

Arthur then gave instructions for some of his men to escort what was left of Bordagan's men from the hills, and to take them far away in the opposite direction, to where the evil butcher had ridden. Volunteers were recruited. Some of Aldfrid's men raised their hands for this duty, and were welcomed.

Bordagan's men were stripped of everything but the clothes they stood up in. No weapons, not even a dagger for protection, were left on their person. The head count showed there were just seventy four of them left. There were some who had been too badly wounded to move, and they were to remain in Aldfrid's care until they were well enough to be sent away.

It was decided that the escort party would leave immediately and would walk all that night and half the following day. They were to follow the road to York and leave them the following noon. All the escorts would be on horseback and heavily armed with crossbows, as well as their swords and shields. The prisoners would walk the whole way.

They set off as preparations were being made for the night's feasting. Arthur had his men use food collected from Bordagan's, camp as well as food of his own. There were a lot of mouths to be fed that night and a victory to be celebrated. The people of the moor brought out lutes and pipes, and music was made.

The night was fine, and the tents of Arthur's camp had been brought and erected on the lower reaches of Great Hill, close to the entrance of Merlin's cave. Great Hill itself was lit all around with beacons and torches. Wood had been collected from some of the settlements that Bordagan had sacked.

Aldfrid declared that new wood would be harvested from trees in the woodland on the edge of Coppice Hill, and that all farms, cottages and bothies that had been destroyed would be rebuilt.

The celebrations went on into the night, until there was hardly anyone left with enough energy to carry on. One by one they retired to their tents, and the people of the hills eventually went back to the caves that had become their homes during Bordagan's time on the hills.

As morning broke, no one rushed to make a move. Arthur eventually gave orders to strike the camp and pack everything onto the carts, ready for moving. There were some tired men that day and every chore was painful, but Arthur had spoken and his orders were obeyed.

Chapter 15

Leaving the Great Moor

Alice and Seth still had not received any instruction from anyone of how they were to return. The last time this had happened to Seth, he simply returned as mysteriously as he had arrived, but he knew this was different, and it worried him.

'Come, we must speak again with Merlin before it is too late and he is gone with Arthur.' The sense of urgency in his voice left an impression on Alice, and they went off to find Merlin.

The entrance to his cave was still open and they went in, calling his name. When they reached the main cavern, they found Merlin sitting talking to Eida.

'I was expecting you,' said Merlin. 'I know why you are here. I have been speaking with Eida about your problem. There is only one thing you can do, and that is return to the great wood—the wood you call Tockholes Wood. But I fear you may be in danger going there. Arthur thinks that is where Bordagan has gone.'

Seth held up his hand. 'It all makes sense now. Bordagan is wounded, and yet it is his spirit that haunts the wood. It is there that all the evil dwells, and we must rid the wood of Bordagan's spirit if we are ever to have any peace. We must return, but how?' he said.

'Come with me, Eida,' said Merlin, looking at the old woman.

The four of them stood, and followed Merlin further into the deep cave. Carrying torches, they went down a long and dark passage that went for what seemed like an eternity until they entered a cavern with a lake in the middle, but this lake was dark. The water was as black as the night.

Seth looked at Alice, and they both had the same thoughts. This was the cavern that Will Strong had spoken of that had been full of evil and darkness.

'Do not be afraid. I know you're of a mind that this place is a bad place. On the contrary, it is a place of great magic. Bathe in these waters and you will be free of Bordagan's hold on you. You will return to your own place and in the time from which you have travelled. When you do return, be sure to do only what is good and right. Do this, and you will rid that place of Bordagan's evil for ever.' Merlin pointed at the black murky waters.

'Go and wash yourselves in the waters, and be free of Bordagan.' Eida nodded her approval at Merlin's instruction.

Seth looked at Alice and then walked into the lake. Alice followed. The water was freezing, and immediately took their breath away.

'You must immerse your heads in the water for it to have the effect,' said Merlin.

Both of them crouched down and allowed their heads to go under the water, then stood quickly and walked out of the lake. As they left the water, a strange feeling came over both of them. They were warm, and their clothes had dried as fast as they had become wet. Alice looked at Seth. Both of them knew that something quite amazing had taken place here. Merlin and Eida smiled.

'Now you, old woman. You, too, enter the lagoon and reap the rewards of these magical waters.' Eida had no idea what Merlin had in mind for her, but she did as was asked of her. She, too, walked in and immersed herself fully under the water, letting out a slight whimper as the cold water took away her breath.

She rose and walked out of the water. Her clothes became dry, and the welcome feeling of warmth was with her also. Seth and Alice looked at her and then took a step towards her. They held the torch closer. Gone were all the lumps and warts that had covered her face. Her hair was fair and long and tidy. She looked years younger.

Merlin turned and walked back in the direction of the long tunnel, back towards his cave. Once back in the main cavern, he pointed towards what appeared to be a table. Laid upon it were a box, and his long staff, which he had made from blackthorn. It was the long and twisted one that had the carving of a goats head for a handle.

'In years to come, a long time from now, the people of these hills will have need of help. If they are fortunate enough to find their way into this cavern—and only those with good intent will ever find the entrance—they will, with the help these items be granted their wishes. When I leave this cave for the last time, I will seal this place so that it will be there for the ones I speak of.' Merlin turned, towards the cave entrance, indicating for them to leave.

Once outside, Merlin held his staff high and spoke

some words that no one could understand. Then he brought the staff crashing down onto the ground. The gorse that had been covering the entrance to the cave quickly spread over the entrance and spread even further, completely hiding the entrance.

All the people of the moors had gathered to see Arthur and his army off. Merlin turned to them and held his staff high once more. He waved it over them.

'After I have left these hills, you will all remember my being here, but none of you will remember where my cave was. Inside, there are some things that your children or your children's children may have great need of, but these things are for their time, not yours. From this moment, you will remember only me.' Again, he waved his staff.

Everyone cheered, and he thanked them for their kindness. On the hill above them, Arthur was sitting on his horse. His men were ready. Merlin walked up to the top of Great Hill and was helped onto a waiting horse.

Arthur's eyes met with Aldfrid's. He sat up straight on his horse and saluted him with his arm across his chest. Aldfrid returned the salute. These were two men with totally different views of life and religion, but who had stood together and fought together for the common good of their peoples.

Arthur then gave a nod to his knights, and the call to move was given. All the men and the carts full of equipment began the long journey south. They had left the large catapults and crossbows for Aldfrid to use as he wished.

That night, after dark, the escort party arrived

back on the hills. Arthur's men and those of Aldfrid's were welcomed, taken into the caves and fed before they settled down for the night. Arthur's men would leave early the following morning to catch up with Arthur and the rest of the main party.

They told Aldfrid that they had left Bordagan's men on the far side of the Pennine Hills, heading in the direction of York.

'They were shattered and feeling very forlorn, and definitely not in the mood for any more fighting. By the time we left them, they were practically on their knees. They will sleep tonight and most of tomorrow,' said the leader of the escort party, whose name was Simon. Everyone laughed, but it was ... a laugh more of relief than of spite. At last the moors were free of Bordagan and his hoard of cut-throats.

Alice and Seth, who were also in the caves and preparing to settle down for the night, had spoken with Aldfrid and told him what Merlin had said to them.

'We will leave in the morning and make our way back. If what Merlin has said will happen does happen, then we shall return safely to our own time,' said Seth. Alice nodded her agreement.

'I wish you well, and I hope you find your way back. If you are able to bring lasting peace to these hills; it would be wonderful. Please tell your people of us and of your time here with us.' Aldfrid smiled, and held out his hand to both Seth and Alice. They took it and shook it warmly.

'Rest assured, sire, we will tell them of all that has gone on here in the name of peace,' Alice told him.

'What are your plans now that the moors are safe?' Seth asked Aldfrid.

'We will begin in the morning to rebuild all the farmsteads and cottages and bothies that Bordagan destroyed. We have friends who have offered to help us with our animal stocks. That will take time, but we will recover.'

They left Aldfrid's chambers and went back to their own small alcove for the night, but before they lay down, Eida came to see them.

'Take me back with you, to your time,' she asked.

'Oh, dear Eida, I wish we could, but it will not be possible. You are not from that time and it doesn't work like that. If it did, we would take you all with us,' said Seth, putting his arm around Eida.

Eida was disappointed, but she accepted what Seth told her. She said she would stay with them that night and see them off in the morning.

The morning arrived and Seth was up and preparing to set off. Alice heard him and also got up. After washing, she and Seth and Eida, who had joined them, ate a hearty breakfast that had been prepared for them by the women.

They were given provisions for their journey and fresh dry pelts of wolf fur to protect them from the cold.

'How long will it take you to return to your time?' asked Aldfrid.

'Tockholes Wood is where we need to go. It was in that wood that our world changed, so if we can get back there, hopefully we will go back to our own time. The only fear is that Bordagan will have gone there, and we don't know what may happen if he has, but Merlin has told us that we will be all right, and I trust him,' Seth said.

There was no more time to be wasted. The three of them made their way out of the cave, followed by Aldfrid, Will Strong and many of the others. Outside, the day was fine--Cold, but at least it was dry, and the sun was trying hard to break through the clouds. Handshakes and hugs were given, and even though they were pleased to be heading home at last, there was some feeling of sadness. Alice and Seth had made some good friends, not least Eida.

Aldfrid insisted that some of his men walk part of the way with them, just in case there were any stragglers from Bordagan's men around. Eida walked with them as well.

The path back to the great wood led them down from Round Loaf and up the steep side of Great Hill. Once on top, they turned east, and in the distance they could see the huge Pendle Hill, where Alice had set off from. Her mind drifted back to her cottage in Sabden.

She wondered what would have become of her cat and the other animals. She had been gone now for so much longer than she had thought she would be. She wondered if Master Wilcocks was still caring for her goat and hens, but she knew he was a good man and wouldn't see them starve.

They made their way down the valley and up the steep rise to the top of Great Hill. They eventually made it to the top and stopped. Alice looked back in the direction of Round Loaf. They could see there were still people standing there and waving to them as they looked across. They waved back before walking on.

Walking down the side of Great Hill was so much easier than walking up, and with the sun now shining, the day had a good feeling about it, one of calm and of being safe. The hills felt like a good place to live now. Alice kept looking back, as she knew that, once she was back in her own time, she would have to come back over these hills on her journey to deliver the stones. She wondered just how much they would have changed from this time to hers, and how would the people of the future who lived on these same hills treat her the next time she crossed over here?

Alice and Seth and the party of moorland settlers who had walked with them reached the bottom of the far side of Great Hill. It was time to say goodbye to them. They could see Tockholes Wood far in the distance. It still looked as dark and unwelcoming as the day they had left it.

There were other hills and a valley to cross before they got there, but if all went well, they would reach the wood before nightfall. The thought of spending the night there did not appeal to Alice. Seth, however, could not wait to get back. He wanted to see what magic Merlin had concocted and how it was going to help them.

Alice turned to her friends and saw that Eida was already in tears, so she gave her a hug. Seth shook hands with the others before he, too, gave Eida a hug. Then it was time to go.

'Best not to hang around; it will be almost dark by the time you get back home,' said Seth. Everyone agreed.

More hugs and waves were offered and the two parties went their separate ways. In no time at all, the hill folk looked like dots to Alice as they made their way back up the side of Great Hill. She and Seth had begun to climb the hill back towards Tockholes Wood. It was still about a mile or more away and had now hidden itself from view as they made their way up.

It was mid-afternoon as they began the long walk over the flat part of the moor towards the wood. Alice suggested to Seth that they should stay in the open that night and go into the wood at daybreak the following day. Seth shook his head and laughed.

'No, we will be safer if we go into the wood. Remember, there are a lot of wolves in this time. There are far fewer in the time we have come from, and apart from that, there is no wood for a fire out here on this plain. We must take the chance and go back.' Alice had no choice but to trust Seth, as he was far more used to these parts than she was.

Not very long after, the two of them reached the edge of the wood. It was a dark and fearful place. Just as they took their first steps amongst the trees, they heard the loud howl of a wolf from somewhere deep inside the vast wood.

Seth began to gather some wood. He said they should stay close to the edge of the wood, but out of sight of the open land. As well as gathering wood, he dragged large branches of trees that had fallen and made a makeshift barricade around them, covering it in loose bracken and other debris.

He lit the fire and made sure he had a good stock of wood, enough to last throughout the night.

'When do you think we will know if we are back in our own time?' asked Alice.

'I will be able to tell once we go much deeper into the wood and we find the stream where we first saw Bordagan and his men riding through. I will be able to tell then,' he said.

'Do you think Bordagan is still here in the wood?' asked Alice.

'I am certain of it, but whereabouts is anyone's guess,' said Seth.'The fire should keep away the wolves, but be sure to keep your staff by your side,' he warned.

Darkness soon arrived, and the sound of the wolves did little to relax the pair of them. The night was going to be a long one.

'At least tomorrow we will have daylight and will be able to find our way into the wood, and with luck we will be back where we belong. Have you decided what you are going to do with those stones you have?' asked Seth.

'Yes, I think so. I owe it to the people to do what is right,' she replied.

'And what do you consider to be right?'

'I need to rid this wood of its curses, and most of all, of Bordagan.'

Seth looked at her. He wasn't sure whether or not to be pleased or worried by Alice's answer. She could see the confusion on his face.

'If the Gatekeeper can prove to me that he has access to the other stones, then I will give him the stones that I have. I want him to be able to unlock the curse that Bordagan has on him. But I fear for what will happen to you and to the Gatekeeper if that is done … What will happen to you?' she asked Seth.

'The Gatekeeper believes that if Bordagan's spell is lifted, we will return to our own time and be allowed to carry on living our lives in peace, and that this great wood will be a place of beauty and tranquillity.' As he spoke, another wolf let out a loud howl, and the two of them burst out laughing.

Alice was soon asleep, but Seth just lay there, deep in thought about what the following day would bring. When he did eventually fall asleep, he slept well and was only woken by Alice, who had prepared some food and a hot herbal drink for them both.

Seth suggested that they should stay close to the top outer edge of the wood for a good part of the way, just as they had done when they had been going towards the moor. He hoped he might be able to recognise some of the terrain further on and then they could enter the wood properly, and hopefully find the stream that led through the great wood.

But he warned Alice that he had a feeling Bordagan was still here in these woods somewhere. If he was wounded, he might be resting up somewhere. Then Alice had some thoughts of her own.

'If, as you say, the spirit of Bordagan that is the evil in these woods, might it not be that he died here after his battle on the moors? If that is the case, then we do not have to fear him, only his spirit,' she offered.

Seth thought about it, and then he nodded. 'You could be right, but we have no way of knowing if he is dead or alive. Nor do we know if he was alone or if he had men with him. We must proceed with caution and assume he is still a threat to us.' Alice agreed.

The uncertainty of what might or might not be ahead of them didn't make their journey back into the wood any easier, and as Seth led the way that morning, Alice stayed close by him. They must have walked along the outer edge of the wood for a good hour or more before Seth stopped suddenly.

'I think this is the place from where we started. I recognise the hill over yonder. If I am right, the cave we sheltered in on that first night is just down here a way.' He pointed down and to the right in the wood.

Then he walked off in that direction. He was right. They soon arrived at the entrance of the cave, but didn't go in. From there Seth turned again and walked back before making his way downhill, deeper into the wood. Alice followed wherever he went; all she could do was trust Seth's judgment.

Not long after, they heard the sound of running water.

'Listen,' said Seth. 'Water. It must be the stream.'

Alice could see the relief on Seth's face. They both quickened their pace and made for where the sound was coming from. Sure enough, it was the stream in which they had hidden from Bordagan.

As soon as they found a place where it was shallow enough, they crouched down and began to fill their water bottles.

'Does this mean we are back in our own time?' asked Alice as she filled her bottle.

'I'm not sure. I will have to have a good look around to see if I recognise the lay of the land,' Seth replied.

'Well, be very sure, my friend. You are not in your own time,' came a voice from behind them on the top of the bank. They both spun round to see the imposing figure of Bordagan standing above them. He was alone and leaning heavily on his pikestaff. In his other hand he held his sword. His neck and tunic were covered in blood. He had been badly wounded in the battle on the moor.

'You—woman—bring fresh water and come up here and dress my wounds,' he ordered.

'I will do no such thing,' replied Alice.

'You dare to disobey me? I will carve your liver and feed it to the wolves.' Bordagan's voice was full of anger, and as he spoke, he spat blood. He was obviously bleeding inside.

Alice and Seth made their way to the top of the banking. Alice stared at Bordagan, and smiled.

'You are finished. This is your last battle and I am your final adversary,' she said. Seth looked at her. He thought she was mad for speaking like that to this butcher of a man.

Hearing what she said made Bordagan laugh, but as he did he coughed, and more blood poured from his mouth.

'See what I mean, Bordagan? You are doomed. You will die here and your soul will never rest.' The more she thought about her choice of words, the more she realised that she might be the one who had cast the curse of Bordagan over these woods and hills. She stopped what she was saying, but it was too late. The words had been spoken.

Bordagan raised his pikestaff and made to strike

out at Seth and Alice. Alice immediately raised her hand and held it out towards him. He stopped dead in his tracks as if he was frozen to the spot. Then slowly he began to fall down. He went onto his knees before steadying himself and eventually sitting upright against a tree trunk. He looked Alice squarely in the eye, smiled at her and slowly closed his eyes.

'He's gone,' said Seth.

'I fear it might be I who have cursed these woods and moors by words' Alice looked at Seth with a look of concern etched on her face.

'I doubt that very much. He was just an evil man,' Seth assured Alice.

While standing looking at the body of Bordagan, wondering if they should attempt to bury him, a wind blew up from nowhere. Then a mist rose from where Bordagan's body sat in the mist, and as it spiralled upwards, round and round, they could make out Bordagan's image. It was his spirit, leaving the corpse. Alice gasped and Seth took a step backwards. Neither of them had seen anything like this before.

The misty spectre of Bordagan's ghost swirled and swirled above them for a minute or two, and suddenly there was a deafening roar. The ground shook and the wind howled through the tree tops.

Seth and Alice crouched down and huddled together, half out of fear but mainly for protection against the wind, which was causing branches to fall from the trees, and the dust that was whipping up like a sandstorm.

When all had calmed down and the ghost of

Bordagan had faded away and gone, they stood up and looked again at his body. But before they could speak about what to do with him, the ground opened up and his body sank down, swallowed up and devoured. The last to go was the gold handle of his sword as it disappeared into the earth. The hole covered itself as quickly as it had appeared, leaving no trace on the ground. It was as if no one had been there.

'Come, quickly, let's get away from here. This is truly an evil place,' said Seth. He took Alice by the hand and they ran away from the stream and went deep into the woods. As they ran, Seth was saying things like, 'This way, and down there.' Alice shouted at him to stop, and he did.

'You are giving instructions as if you know where you are,' she said.

'I hadn't given it a thought. He looked around, and said, 'We are back in our time. I do recognise this place.' He was jumping for joy!

'Now we have to face the Gatekeeper, when we find him or he finds us; we will have some explaining to do. He will be annoyed that we have been away so long and still haven't brought the stones back with us,' said Alice.

'But you know where the stones are, don't you? We can go and get them now, before we see the Gatekeeper, if you prefer,' said Seth.

'I think, in light of all that has happened, we should wait to see his reaction at what has happened to us. I want to explain what I intend to do with the stones, but if he objects, then I will have a problem on my hands.'

'What will happen to you if all does not go well with what I have to say to him? We have become good friends, but I fear the spell he holds over you may prove stronger than our friendship,' said Alice.

Seth's bowed his head. He didn't have an answer for her. He knew the strength of the Gatekeeper and the power he had over him. He could turn him from the big strapping man who had helped Alice through so much over the past few days into the snivelling, warped Dregs, at his will. Alice touched Seth's arm gently, letting him know she understood.

'Let's not worry about that until we have to,' she said.

Soon, Seth had found the path that led to the Gatekeeper's house, and reluctantly they made their way along it. The wood still had a feeling of unease and darkness about it. and Alice suspected it would remain like that for as long as Bordagan—or his spirit—had a hold over the place.

After a while they could see the Gatekeepers house in the distance, with smoke rising from its stack. Seth stopped and looked at Alice. She took hold of his hand.

'Be brave. Soon all will be well.' Nodding her head, she smiled at him reassuringly. He returned her smile.

'You're back so soon!' said a voice from behind them. It was the Gatekeeper.

Alice thought he was being sarcastic.

'To have been gone less than an hour, you must have had the stones very close by. Where are they? Show them to me.' he demanded.

Less than an hour? What are you talking about?'

asked Alice.

'Enough! Give me the stones,' he demanded again. By now the Gatekeeper was becoming very agitated.

Seth and Alice looked at one another. 'Master, a most peculiar thing has happened to us since we left here. You must allow us to explain.' said Seth.

'If this is some trickery…' The Gatekeeper was beginning to twitch, and his head was shaking.

'Rest assured, it is not trickery of any kind. Just allow us to explain and all will be well, I give you my word,' said Alice.

'The word of a witch, and what worth is that to me? If I find you have betrayed me, I will deliver the two of you to Sir Thomas myself, and I will take pleasure in watching you burn side by side.' His mouth twisted, and he spat as he spoke. There was such venom in his tone. 'Now let me hear what this witch has to say.'

Alice was unperturbed by him; she had a new confidence about her. The three of them walked to the front of the house and sat down outside. Seth began trying to explain about hearing the horses coming and then finding himself and Alice back in the time of Arthur and Merlin, and how they had been gone for over a week and that they had come back here only to be confronted by Bordagan as he lay dying. He stuttered and stammered and spoke so fast. Alice stopped him.

'What Seth is trying to tell you is the truth. When we left you to go and fetch the stones, we found ourselves in a very peculiar time slip.' The Gatekeeper looked at them. It was obvious he didn't believe a word of it.

'We had gone back in time to when Merlin stayed on these hills, and we became caught up in a huge battle. It was Bordagan's trickery that took us back. He wanted us to help him find Merlin, but we didn't. We did meet Merlin with the help of the people of the moors, and Merlin has given me the power to help you to be free of this curse that holds you here. If you will trust me, I can rid you of the hold that Bordagan has over both you and Seth, but you must trust me.' Seth looked at the Gatekeeper and nodded …

'It is true what she says, master. All of it is the truth,' said Seth.

'You say you want the stones. What do you want them for? What power do you hope to get from having them?' Alice asked the Gatekeeper.

'The power to free myself of this curse and to be more powerful than Bordagan so he cannot keep me as his slave in this place,' he said.

'Then we both want the same thing. The only difference is, I will rid the world of Bordagan's spirit. This whole place will have peace if we do it my way,' said Alice.

The Gatekeeper thought for a moment. He stood up and walked around with his head down.

'How do I know what you say is the truth?' he asked.

Then Seth stood up. 'Look!' He held up the wolf pelt that he still had around his shoulders. By some strange stroke of luck, they still had them, even back here in this time.

'How do you explain us having these pelts? No

one has wolf pelts today. We were given these by the people of the moor.'

'That is true. Where do you think we would get these from? Certainly not in these woods and in only one hour of leaving you,' she told the Gatekeeper.

The Gatekeeper scratched his head and thought some more. He was finding it hard to believe, and difficult to take in, but deep down he knew the power of Bordagan's magic and the way he could move people around in time. After all, he had done it with him and with Seth.

He stopped, and looked at the pair of them sitting there on a log.

'Very well, I believe you. What is your plan of action?' he asked Alice.

Alice reminded him that he had said he knew where the other three stones of Merlin were. She said she needed them all to be together for Merlin's magic to be strong enough to work. The Gatekeeper hesitated.

'Well, do you know where the other runes are?' asked Alice.

'Yes, I know who has them, but getting them will not be easy,' he replied.

'They are in the possession of two of Lancaster's most prominent families. Two are in the possession of the De Hoghtons at Hoghton Tower. I believe they are hidden behind a fireplace in the great hall. The one at Samlesbury is in a burial vault behind the hall, and both are guarded well. The two families do not get on with each other, or amongst themselves. Each suspects the other is trying to steal the stones,' said the Gatekeeper.

'How did you find out about this?' asked Alice.

'I was told by your friend, Mistress Preston of Pendle. It was she who suggested you should be the one to deliver the stones to Cedric Hoghton. He is a distant relative of the De Hoghtons, but he doesn't see eye to eye with them. He, too, wants the stones. They all think they can do so much if they have them, but Mistress Preston has helped me in the past. She told me you were the only person strong-willed enough to be able to carry this task through. I was to take the stones from you and then find a way of acquiring the other three. Will you help me to lay my hands on the others?' He looked at her almost pleadingly.

Alice had heard of the feud between the two families, but she had no idea that they were involved with owning the runes of Merlin. The Gatekeeper explained that Mistress Preston had been friends with one of the members of the family from Samlesbury Hall, and had been told of the power that the stones had. She had come across the two that Alice had been delivering by way of a favour from a gardener at Clitheroe Castle, where they had been kept.

It all made sense now. Alice had wondered why she had been told to travel this long way over the moors, but had not questioned it at the time. There was no turning back now. She had to see this through. And rather than hand the stones to some families, whose feud looked like it would go on for years, she knew it was better to try to bring peace to the woods and moors that had become so much a part of her life over the past week.

'I will help you,' she said. 'I have an idea that might work, but I will need Seth to help me.' The Gatekeeper agreed.

It would be half a day's walk to the tower at Hoghton and another hour further on to Samlesbury Hall. She thought it better to wait until the following day and then put her plan into action. The days were getting shorter as the year wore on, and it was easier to make their way overland in the daylight than in the darkness, especially with having to cross the river at Hoghton Bottoms. There was a bridge, but it would mean a slight detour.

That night, the Gatekeeper showed that he did have a kinder side to his demeanour. He provided food and warm beds for Alice and for Seth. Before bedtime, Alice told them what her plan was and how she hoped it would work in their favour.

'I will go with Seth as far as Hoghton Tower. It should take Seth another hour to make his way to the hall at Samlesbury. When I think he has arrived at his destination, I will find a barn or some other outbuilding and set a fire. At the same time, Seth should do the same. We will then draw attention to the fire by throwing stones through the windows of the house.

'The occupants will come out, see the fire and run to put out the flames. While they are doing that, we will go to where the stones are hidden and take them. It is my guess that each family will blame the other for the fire and also for the theft of the stones, once they notice them missing. They will challenge each other and leave us alone to return here under the cover of darkness,' said Alice.

Seth and the Gatekeeper agreed that this might work, providing they could find the stones' hiding place. Neither of them had been to these houses before, and they had no idea of the layout of the houses. All they knew was that they were very grand places. The Gatekeeper could offer no help with this kind of information, as he had never left the woods since being cursed by Bordagan.

'What if we can't find the stones?' asked Seth.

'We will find them, I know we will. Remember Merlin's words after we bathed in the freezing black lagoon? His magic washed over us that day. We must have faith, and all will be well.' Her words cheered Seth. The Gatekeeper had no idea what they were talking about, but he felt he could trust them.

Alice and Seth slept better that night than they had done for ages. They woke feeling completely refreshed. It was daylight when Alice walked out of the house. The Gatekeeper was busy chopping wood round the side of the house.

'You do realise that once I have all five of the runes of Merlin, I can use them how I wish, and it is my wish to rid this wood and the moors of any hold or evil spell that Bordagan has upon them and anyone living here? I worry about how you and Seth will be affected by my actions,' said Alice.

'Please do not concern yourself. Once the evil of Bordagan is defeated, I and poor Seth will be at peace. We will be with our families, and we will have returned to live our lives as they should be lived, in our own times. I wish for nothing more. I have hated this existence. I have wreaked misery on so many poor souls, not because I wanted to, but because I couldn't help it. I was no more than an extension of Bordagan's evil. When he is gone, so I will be gone, and so will all the evil that haunts these woods.' Alice was relieved to hear the Gatekeeper's wishes. It made her want her task to be a success all the more.

Seth joined them, and they sat and ate bread, salted pork and eggs, along with a hot herbal brew. By now, Alice was eager to get on and begin the walk overland to Hoghton.

Chapter 16

Uniting the Runes of Merlin

Alice and Seth set off in the direction of Hoghton Tower with about six hours of daylight remaining. Their plan was to reach the tower with an hour of light left. That would give Seth enough time get across the river and make his way to Samlesbury Hall.

They would then wait until they could see the candles extinguished, which would mean everyone had retired to bed, and then they would light their fires and hopefully complete their mission. After they would find a spot that was away from any main paths and hide there until the other had returned.

The walk to the tower wasn't so hard, and they arrived earlier than they had expected to. They had been able to follow the coach road, but hid when a coach came past them on its way to Preston. The only other people they saw were a traveller and a man cutting hedgerows. Alice and Seth could see the long lane leading up to the tower as they got nearer to it.

The tower itself was hidden in a large wood on top of a hill. The hillside was also covered with lots of trees and undergrowth. This was perfect for Alice, as it meant she would be able to approach the tower unseen.

When they arrived at the gate at the end of the lane, it was too early for Alice to attempt to make her way nearer to the tower, as there would be groundsmen still working as long as it was daylight. They walked past the entrance and down to a lane on the right about a quarter of a mile further on. There, they hid in bushes for a while until the light began to fade.

When they thought it was late enough, Seth left Alice and began to make his way over the fields towards Hoghton Bottoms and the bridge across the river. Alice stayed in the bushes until it was dark, and then she set off back towards the lane end for the tower.

Walking through the gateway, she turned left into the bushes and the cover they would provide for her. The walk up to the tower itself was much further than she had thought. On her way up, she heard voices and laughter coming towards her. They were estate workers. She crouched down and kept still until they had gone well past.

Eventually, she arrived at the tower itself. It was a huge imposing structure. Through the gate she could make out a courtyard with buildings on all sides. She walked around the side of the outer wall and looked for a building that would suit her purpose. It wasn't long before she found one. There was a big hay barn that was well-stocked with animal feed for the winter months. This would burn well, she thought to herself, and with any luck the fire would be seen for miles around, maybe even as far as Samlesbury Hall.

Alice waited for a while longer, hiding herself well out of the way in case any members of staff or even the gentry came along. It was a cold night, but dry. There was no sign of a moon or stars, which was a good thing, as at least the darkness would aid their escape once the deed had been done.

Neither Alice nor Seth knew for sure when the other would begin the fun and games. It was a case of doing it when they thought the house had retired for the night. All they could do was hope that both families would go to bed around the same time.

Seth had arrived at his destination in good time. He had no trouble finding the bridge over the river and was now waiting, just like Alice was. He had sneaked around the grounds and found a stable with six horses bedded down for the night. He decided he would let the horses loose and then set the stable on fire. He had also found the burial chambers, which were set away from the house, and luckily they were away from the stables, which were to the rear of the house. There was a fence around the chamber, but Seth didn't envisage it causing him any problems.

From where Seth was, he could see the lights inside the house. There were two sets of lights. Seth had it in his mind that one set of lights must have been the servants' quarters, and the others were where the family lived. The first to go out were the ones he thought were the family's. Almost straight after, the other lights were also extinguished.

That was Seth's signal to be ready to act. He waited a while longer and then crept around to the stables. He lifted the latch on the door and went in. The horses were all tethered in their own boosts. One by one, and with calmness, Seth unfastened the harnesses that were holding the horses, and set them free.

He had left the stable door open, and first one and

then another found their way out into the yard. They made no fuss. All was done quietly and calmly. When the last of the horses had left, Seth lit his fire. There was a lot of hay and straw in the stable, and above was a loft containing lots more.

He knew that when the horses smelled the smoke they would become very lively and make a lot of noise before bolting away. This was his time to leave and go round to the front of the house. He would have to make enough noise to waken the inhabitants before going round to the burial chamber and to where the runes were kept. His main hope was that he could find the runes and make good his escape without being seen. Excitement filled him as adrenaline rushed through his veins.

He piled up lots of dry straw against the wall under the loft and set it burning, before running out and stirring up the horses. Next he ran around to the front of the house and threw three or four large stones through the windows nearest to the main door.

He didn't wait for any lights. He quickly made his way to the back of the house and to the burial chambers. He climbed the fence and looked for an entrance to the chamber. There were huge stones on top of the oblong chamber. There was no other way in.

Despite being a big man, Seth knew he wouldn't be able to move those stones on his own. But something inside him was telling him to try. A voice in his head kept saying. 'You can do this.' He looked at the huge stones, and bending down, he heaved at one of them. To his surprise, it moved quite easily.

He thought of Merlin's words and knew this was his doing.

He made enough room to squeeze through, and dropped down inside the chamber. Inside, it was far bigger than it appeared above ground. There were a number of caskets in there, all of which were on plinths, and around the sides were shelves. Seth had made a makeshift torch out of hay from the stables. He lit it and looked around. There, on one of the shelves, was a glass case with a single triangular granite stone inside …

This had to be it, he thought to himself. He looked around again, but couldn't see anything else that resembled anything like a rune. He lifted the case and picked up the stone. Placing it in his pocket, he climbed up out of the chamber and slid the huge covering slab back into place.

By now there was a lot of noise coming from the side of the house. The stables were well alight. Keeping down and out of sight, he could see through the light of the fire that some of the servants were trying to douse the flames. They had made a human chain along with members of the house and were fetching buckets from a well in the grounds. One young lad was doing his best to round up the horses.

Seth left them to their troubles and headed away from the house, making for a hedgerow some fifty yards away. This would provide cover for him to begin his journey back to where he had left Alice some hours earlier. Back at Hoghton Tower, Alice was creating mischief of her own, not too dissimilar to Seth's.

She, too, had waited for all the lights in the house

to go out, but before lighting a fire, she wandered into the courtyard and looked for a place to hide. Her plan was to start her fire then to raise the alarm the same way Seth had done, but she needed a place close to the house entrance, so she could enter and find the great hall and hopefully the two runes.

There was a low wall below the steps that led up to the main door. It had a balustrade along the top, but it wasn't very high and would hardly provide any cover at all. The only other hiding place was across the courtyard, but she would be exposed as she made her way across to the entrance. She felt her best option was to hide behind the low wall and hope that the commotion of the fire would distract any attention away from her.

When the time came, Alice was around the back of the main wall, behind the barn that was to be her distraction. She watched for the lights going out, waited a short while and was about to make her move. Suddenly, she could see a glow in the distance from the hilltop where Hoghton Tower stood. The glow got bigger and bigger. Alice smiled to herself; she knew that was Seth at work.

It was time to act. She did exactly what Seth had done down at Samlesbury Hall. She piled a lot of loose straw where she knew it would cause the fire to spread, and then lit it.

Without any hesitation, she hurried around to the front of the house. She waited a while until the flames had well and truly taken hold and the fire could easily be seen from the main house, then she threw stones through the front windows.

Alice crouched down, pulling her black cape

over her head to hide her in the darkness, and she waited. She heard the bolt slide open and the latch on the heavy wooden door lift, before an army of people, servants and members of the household came rushing out.

Some were shouting 'Fire!' while others were giving instructions to bring pails of water. Some of the women were screaming, but all ran down the steps and away from where Alice was crouched down. As the last of them ran out of the courtyard, Alice made her way up the steps and through the open door of the house. Opening door after door, she eventually found the great hall.

Inside was a long solid wood banqueting table. It was clearly a house of high standing, and the people who lived there must have been high-ranking in the royal court. All around the sides were shields bearing coats of arms, accompanied by armaments of every description. There were trophies of animals' heads on wooden plaques hung on the walls, and paintings of noblemen; probably family members, thought Alice.

There was a huge open fireplace, large enough to roast an ox in. All around the sides of the great hall were various glass cabinets. Alice looked in them all, searching for the two runes. Eventually, she found them. They had been placed in a silver box within one of the glass cases. She removed them as quickly and quietly as she could.

She now had to find her way back out of the maze of passageways that had brought her to the great hall. She thought she knew where to go. She turned left and down a long corridor, but she didn't recognise any of the places it led her to. She went back and tried another way, but again this led to nowhere. Then she heard voices. Surely they could not have put out that fire so soon.

Alice slipped into one of the rooms and waited. Two men came running down the passage, past where she was and into the great hall. Within seconds they came out again carrying muskets, swords and other weapons. She heard one of the men saying, 'They will pay for this.'

Alice quietly opened the door and watched the two men leave. She followed them at a distance, and finally found her way out. As she reached the door, four horsemen rode into the courtyard along with two spare horses. The two men mounted up, and all six rode out together. The rest of the servants and family were still fighting to put out the fire. Alice looked at the flames as they leaped high into the night sky, and knew they were fighting a losing battle. As stealthily as she had got there, she left. As she began to make her way downhill, away from the house, she stayed hidden amongst the trees. She watched the six horsemen riding own the hill towards the gate, and wondered if the plan had worked. Had they thought it was the work of the feuding family from Samlesbury Hall, and vice versa?

Now she had to get back to where she had left Seth and hope that all had gone as well for him as it had for her. The journey back to meet Seth was far easier than the long climb up to the tower, and it didn't seem to take her as long. When she got back to the lane end, Seth was already waiting for her.

'Did you get the stones?' he asked.

'Yes. Did you manage to get yours?' she asked him.

He nodded, 'With a little help from Merlin, I did.' He explained about the huge stone slabs, and the two of them laughed. 'I have just seen six horsemen galloping hard down this lane, coming from your direction. Did you see them?' he asked.

Alice explained who they were and how she had almost been caught by two of them as they came into the house to collect weapons, and how they had cursed, saying they would make someone pay. It looked as though they did blame the family from Samlesbury Hall.

Wasting no more time, the two of them began the long walk back to Tockholes Wood. It had been a long day, and night, and they were both incredibly tired. The walk back was uninterrupted, but seemed to be much harder than the walk to the tower, mainly because going back was all uphill.

It was the middle of the night when they reached the wood. Alice wondered if the Gatekeeper would be waiting for them, and she suspected he would be. He would probably be unable to sleep for wondering if they had been successful in finding the stones.

She asked Seth if he thought the Gatekeeper could be trusted. Seth looked at her. He hadn't really considered that. He asked what she meant.

'I mean, if he knows we have all the stones, will he go along with what we had agreed, or do you think he might try to take them and use them for his own ends?' Said Alice.

Seth stopped and wondered about this.

'Now that you mention it, I have never known him to keep his word to anyone about anything. The evil in him overrides anything good. In the past, he has always taken what he wants. He never gives a quarter. What are you going to do?' he asked Alice.

'I think you should walk on alone for a while and give me time to think,' she replied

Seth suspected Alice was going to stash the stones somewhere for safekeeping. Although he was the Gatekeeper's servant, he didn't trust him, nor did he owe him any favours. He agreed with Alice's suggestion, and walked on ahead alone. He kept walking, and out of respect for Alice and the good she was trying to do, he didn't look back once to see what she was doing.

After a while, she caught up with him.

'Everything all right?' he asked.

'Everything's is fine,' said Alice. They walked on together.

They hadn't even reached the path that led down to the Gatekeeper's house when he met them. He walked towards them, holding a torch. They could see he was anxious to know how they had fared.

'Did you get them?' he asked. 'Well, did you?' He was becoming very agitated.

'Yes, we got them,' answered Alice.

He relaxed at hearing the news. Seth kept quiet and didn't make eye contact with his master. He knew his moods and didn't want to become too optimistic about what might happen.

'Show them to me,' the Gatekeeper demanded. The tone of his voice was curt and not like that of the man who had seen them off on their mission the afternoon before.

'You sound rather impatient, Gatekeeper. Is there something troubling you?' enquired Alice.

Seth lowered his gaze even further, fearing Alice's questions would anger his master. He knew only too well how savagely the man could react to anyone who had the nerve to stand up to him.

'Hand me the stones, let me see them,' he roared at Alice. His eyes were again turning blood red with temper.

Alice stood and looked at him. She also looked at Seth, who was virtually cowering as he began to back away from the two of them. He was clearly frightened of the confrontation between them.

'Gatekeeper, do you not trust me? Don't you remember we made a pact over what we would do with the stones if we could get all five of them?' she said. 'Your mood suggests to me that you are about to break that agreement.' Alice stood firm and showed no fear. Then she turned to Seth.

'What do you fear, Seth? Do you not remember Merlin's words?' She reminded him, 'we were washed in the deep lagoon and have no need to fear anyone or spells or acts of evil again. No one can harm you anymore.' Seth didn't seem convinced.

'Merlin cannot help you here. I have the power in this place,' said the Gatekeeper as he darted towards Seth, grabbing him by the shoulder. Despite his huge frame, Seth was clearly scared. It quickly became a battle of who could convince Seth the most.

'Resist him, Seth. Stand up against him; he cannot harm you anymore, he cannot control you if you resist him,' said Alice.

'Go, take the stones from her now or feel my wrath,' said the Gatekeeper to Seth as he pushed him towards Alice. Alice lifted her hand and touched Seth's shoulder. Seth stopped, appearing to regain his composure. Her touch had restored his strength and courage.

'What magic is this? I command you to do my bidding, or I will turn you into Dregs and leave you like that for all time.'

'Be strong, Seth. He cannot harm you if you remain strong, and remember Merlin's words,' said Alice.

The Gatekeeper made another move towards Seth, who was now standing shoulder to shoulder with Alice. Alice raised her hand and held it out towards the Gatekeeper. He stopped, and looked bemused. He cursed Seth, condemning him to be Dregs, but it did no good. Seth remained Seth. Much to his surprise, Merlin's words and spells had worked. As Seth realised this, his confidence grew, and he began to smile in defiance at the Gatekeeper.

'I need those stones. Give them to me, or I will turn the two of you into stones, like the ones near to you.'

Alice looked around. There were indeed large rocks nearby. She wondered if these had once been people who might have betrayed the Gatekeeper, but his words did nothing to unnerve her. 'Be warned— Merlin has given us protection against evil. You cannot tell us what to do anymore. Now, you either keep the promise you made to me and help us to rid this wood and everything about it of the evil that Bordagan holds over you, or I will simply go ahead and do it myself. I am doing this for Seth. He is a good man who does not deserve this,' said Alice.

The Gatekeeper raised his staff and brought it down hard on the ground … Thump! Then he looked behind him. Out of the darkness of the trees came a growl and a rustling of bushes. Suddenly, two sets of bright yellow eyes, glowing like nothing either Alice or Seth had ever seen before, came rushing at them with incredible speed. Seth stepped back, but Alice stood her ground.

She was shocked, but only for a split second. Then she raised her own staff. There in front of them were two of the biggest wolves ever. Seeing Alice's staff held high, they stopped and just stood by the Gatekeeper, snarling and frothing at the mouth.

'I will give you one last chance. Give me those runes now, or my two friends here will tear you to pieces.'

'There is one slight problem with your plan,' said Alice.

'And what is that?' he asked.

'I do not have the stones on my person; they are in a safe place. You see, I suspected this betrayal from you. If you set your 'dogs' upon us, you will never find out where the runes of Merlin are hidden, and you will be condemned to this life of perpetual hell forever. And apart from that, your two friends are no match for me.' Alice pointed at the two wolves and stared deeply into their eyes.

The snarling stopped as the anger and the brightness left their eyes. They lowered their heads and lay down, placing their gazes on the floor. The Gatekeeper looked down at them, and his anger welled again as he realised he had lost control of the situation. Again, he crashed his staff to the floor.

The two wolves raised their heads, stood and began to growl. Alice lifted her hand, and once again the beasts fell silent. The Gatekeeper gave in. He threw his staff to the ground and held up his arms.

'You said all you wanted was to be returned to your own time and to your family. I am giving you the chance to have all that, so why are you acting like this?' Alice asked him.

'Those runes hold far more power than you think. I can have more than just returning to my family. If you were to join me, we could all have that power, and we could have great riches with such power.' He looked at Alice and Seth, hoping for a favourable response, but Alice just shook her head.

'You are condemned by Bordagan to stay in these woods forever, and only I can free you from that curse. I am the only one who can move freely over these hills. Do you suppose Mistress Preston knew this when she asked me to bring the runes over these hills? You said she is your friend. Perhaps this is her way of trying to help a friend.' Alice looked at him inquiringly, hoping he would see her reasoning.

The Gatekeeper's bowed his head as he contemplated her words. 'But there is so much to be had, don't you see?'

Alice again shook her head. 'Merlin told Seth and me that the runes can only be used for good purposes, but what you are suggesting is not good, it is greed, and your plans are doomed. The best you can hope for is to allow me to rid you and Seth and the whole of this wood and the hills they stand upon from the curse Bordagan has placed here. I will do that for you, but you must stop trying to fight me. This is all for good, and it is the only thing that will work,' Alice said.

He knew he was defeated. He bent down and picked up his staff. Raising it high and bringing it down across his knee, he broke the staff in two. As the Gatekeeper did this, the two wolves that had been at his side ran off back into the trees, whimpering as they went.

'Very well, do what you have to do,' said the Gatekeeper.

Alice told Seth not to be afraid of the Gatekeeper anymore, and said she needed him to stay with him and make sure he used no more trickery until she had collected the runes and united them all together. He agreed.

By now, daylight was beginning to break through the tops of the tree tops The Gatekeeper suggested they eat before Alice left to collect the runes. They had travelled all night, and the last bite they had had was when they were waiting for darkness to fall the night before. They made their way back to the Gatekeeper's house, which wasn't very far. There was a warm fire burning, and hot herbal drinks were served. Seth looked at Alice, offering a frown of suspicion at the drink that had been given. He didn't trust the Gatekeeper one inch.

Alice looked into the cup, sniffed it and took a sip. She smiled at Seth. All seemed fine with the drink. The Gatekeeper saw this and laughed quietly, but not quietly enough for them not to notice.

'You really do not trust me at all, do you? Mind you, I wouldn't trust me either. Very few have come through these woods and have not met the dark side of me, no one more than you, eh, Seth? But fear not. I believe that Mistress Preston, who incidentally was one of the more fortunate ones, has sent you on this mission with the purpose of helping me, and having seen your strength, I will go along with all you have in mind. I will not obstruct you anymore, nor will I attempt to harm either of you in your duties,' he said.

Alice thanked him and said she hoped he would not betray them. After their meal, all they wanted to do was sleep. It had been a full day since they had closed their eyes. Seth still didn't trust the Gatekeeper, and told Alice she should sleep, and said he would sleep later. Alice knew why he had said this, but rather than questioning him she just nodded and agreed with him. She told him not to let her sleep for too long. It was important that she left the Gatekeeper's before noon.

Seth kept his word and woke Alice after she had slept for a few hours. It was almost noon as she got up. The rest had been most welcome, but now it was time to put their plan into place. She walked out onto the porch. The Gatekeeper and Seth were both there.

'You know what I have to do. I must take the stones to the place on Great Hill and place them together in unity. I will then ask them to rid these woods and the hills of the evil that is here. You will be with your families again. My dear Seth, we have been on such a journey together. I will never forget you …'

Seth interrupted her. 'But I will be coming with you, wont I?'

'Do you not remember what Merlin said? The stones must be reunited on Great Hill for their magic to work, and you are condemned to remain here, along with the Gatekeeper. You only left before because it suited Bordagan, and because you were in the time slip.'

Then the Gatekeeper spoke. 'He may go with you, but only in the form of Dregs. It was I who cursed him to be this way and held him here in this time, not Bordagan. I have made his plight in such a way that he can roam freely, as long as he is Dregs. Take him with you,' said the Gatekeeper.

Alice looked at Seth. Seth looked at her pleadingly. It was clear he didn't want to stay in this place a moment longer than he had to. 'Very well, if that is what Seth wants,' agreed Alice.

Seth nodded, and then proceeded to hug her. Alice was shocked, as it wasn't the sort of practice she was used to, but she smiled, as it did feel nice to have that friendliness.

The Gatekeeper knew it was time for them to leave. He extended his hand to Alice, and she took it.

'Have a safe journey. If all goes well, I will soon be back with my family. I hope I don't cross paths with Bordagan again,' he said.

Alice assured him that if all went well with reuniting the runes, then Bordagan would never be seen in these parts again. And with that, Alice and Seth began to walk out of the clearing and away from the Gatekeeper's house.

'Have faith, I will not let you down,' said Alice as she looked back at him. He held up his hand and smiled. She could sense his apprehension from the look on his face. She knew she must not let him and Seth down. This wasn't like the Alice Bond that had left Pendle some days earlier. Kindness and consideration had not been her strong points, but events had changed her, and she knew it.

The walk back to where she had hidden the three stones hidden didn't take long. Then she had to find her way to where she had left the original two that she had brought with her over the hills. This was going to take a bit longer than she had thought.

Alice explained to Seth that she had left the two original stones hidden, in a loose stone in the outer wall of the bothy where she had spent her last night before entering Tockholes Wood. Seth warned her that as soon as he stepped out of the wood, he would change and become Dregs.

'Will that present a problem?' she asked him. 'Are you likely to try to take the stones from me once you become Dregs?'

He shook his head and reminded her of the new powers she had acquired since their time with Merlin.

'I feel you will be a match for anyone, and although my form will change, my feelings will not.' Alice wondered what he meant by 'feelings'.

They reached the edge of the great wood, and Alice looked at Seth. Both of them took a deep breath and stepped out of the wood, and as they did so, Seth dropped to his knees and writhed and moaned as his form became twisted and gnarled. Then with a grunt he jumped to his feet. The transformation was over and Seth had become Dregs. Alice looked at him.

'Are you all right?' she enquired.

'Of course I'm all right, woman. Why do you have to always ask such silly questions? I am Dregs, and Dregs is always all right.' He shooed her away towards the broken-down bothy that was in view.

Alice smiled at the abruptness of the scruffy little man who was now her new companion, and then she did as she was told and made towards the bothy.

They were there in no time at all. Alice walked to the side of the building, bent down and began to wrestle with a loose stone. Reaching inside the hole, she pulled out the piece of rag that held the two runes. Now she had all five. At last, and after more than one thousand years, all five runes had been reunited. It was now time to set off on the long walk to Great Hill. Dregs looked at her, and seeing her holding the stones made him dance and jump up and down with excitement.

Chapter 17

The Return to Great Hill

It was now early afternoon, and the November day's weather was worsening, but Alice had decided there was no more time to waste. Even though she had no intention of following her mission through, and delivering the runes to Cedric Hoghton, she was still going to go and see him. What she had in her mind for an explanation, she hadn't yet decided.

Dregs said he thought it would be wiser to go around the edge of the wood rather than go through it, as he still didn't trust the Gatekeeper. There was a huge difference in the distance they would have to walk since the last time they had walked around the edge of Tockholes Wood.

There had been over a thousand years of forestry work carried out, Dregs explained.

'The wood has been cut back by miles in the years since Aldfrid's time, so it will take us only half the time to go round it now. For years and years they took trees away from this vast wood for building. It's still a huge wood, but nowhere near half the size it was.' He said it was only the fear of the Gatekeeper and the evil that he subjected the woodsmen to that finally stopped them harvesting any further.

Even though the wood was much smaller, the day didn't last any longer and darkness was fast approaching well before they had found the edge of the wood. Dregs suggested building a shelter and staying by the edge of the wood for the night. The shelter was to protect them against the elements; at least now they were in their own time there were no wolves to worry about.

Dregs assured Alice that the two terrifying ones the Gatekeeper had tried to scare them with had been nothing more than apparitions. Alice had learned from the farmers around Pendle that the only wolves left were around the middle of England, and maybe a few in the Cheshire area. Most had been killed off over the last fifty years.

By the time night came in, Dregs had built a shelter that would keep out the wind and rain, if any fell. They lit a fire and settled down. They were still very tired from all the efforts of the night before, and both of them were soon fast asleep.

They woke to dark skies and a cold wind. Dregs looked at the sky and grunted.

'Ugh! Not a good day for a walk onto yonder moor, good job we have the wolf pelts … need them today,' he warned Alice.

Alice looked up at the sky. She could see what he meant. The clouds were blacker than she had ever seen storm clouds before. She wasn't sure what the clouds held, be it rain or snow, but they certainly looked menacing indeed.

'True wintery weather clouds, those, Dregs?' she offered. He nodded his agreement.

After having a hot drink and some food, they put out the fire, pulled down the shelter and began the rest of their walk. They didn't have too far to go before the wood turned to the right and fell away downhill. Alice was as surprised as Dregs had said she would be.

'Is this the end of the wood?' she asked.

'Aye … I told ye, din I? Not much left of it now … woodsmen took it all … I told ye.'

Alice had to smile at the way Dregs was, and the way he spoke. He was so different from Seth, but likeable all the same. It was hard to believe that this was really the same man.

From the top of the hill where they were, they could see Great Hill in the distance. It appeared so close, and yet it would be a few hours walk, and all uphill at that. The walk down the hill around the side of Tockholes Wood brought them to a road—quite a wide track. Dregs was quick to explain that this was the stagecoach route from Bolton to Preston.

Once they got across the track, there was a decent path that had been made by travellers who had for years made their way over the moors. This was also used as a shepherds' trail for those taking livestock to markets across the county. It was still quite rough in places, but better than the bogs that Alice had encountered over Darwen Moor.

With half the original wood having been removed over the years, it was so much easier and not as daunting. Slowly, they walked together on to Great Hill. They saw no one on their walk, but could see small houses and farmsteads dotted about the hills; some had smoke rising from their chimney stacks. Some sheep and cattle were grazing.

The weather over this side of the moor had changed. The clouds had broken and had strange, brighter colours. They were greyer and had tinges of blue and pink. They also appeared to be racing across the sky much faster, but as Alice and Dregs looked back at the huge Tockholes Wood, which was now some miles away in the distance, the clouds over the wood were still as black as hell itself.

They made their way to the south side of the hill, where they remembered the entrance to Merlin's cave had been. They walked all the way round, but there was no sign of it anywhere. The landscape had changed so much, but then Dregs remembered.

'Ah! Now I know why we can't find it, I remember now. Din I tell ye? Many years ago, the word was there had been a huge crash and the whole ground had changed, and that's why we can't find it,' he said.

'What are we going to do, then? Merlin said we had to bring the stones back to the cave for the magic to work.' Alice was worried.

'We'll just have to guess. We know it was on this side of the hill, and I can recall it was about half way around the side coming from Eida's place, but Eida aint here no more neither.' Then Dregs looked towards where Eida's tunnel had been, and noticed there was still a row of hawthorn growing.

'That row of hawthorn yonder, do you think that is where Eida was? If it is, then we aren't so far away.' He turned and looked the other way. Alice's eyes followed his. The side of Great Hill, where they had once found the entrance to Merlin's cave, had changed. There were no gorse bushes anymore that had provided the cover for the entrance. All there was now was grass on the hillside, and the odd stone protruding from the ground.

From the side of one of those stones, out popped a

rabbit. It only took a few steps, and then it saw Alice and Dregs and ran back down its hole. Alice looked at Dregs, and he at her. They both had the same thought. Could that be where the cave entrance had once been, and was that rabbit trying to tell them something? It went through Alice's mind that it might even be the work of Merlin himself, offering them a sign.

The two of them smiled, and made towards the rock and the hole that was behind it. It was only a small rabbit hole, certainly not big enough to crawl down or even see down, but this was as near as they were going to get to Merlin's cave, and it would have to do.

'Are you ready, my friend?' Alice asked Dregs.

She could see a tear welling in the corner of his eye, and it made her feel unusually sentimental. He nodded and stood up as she opened her cloth bag and took out the rag containing the five runes of Merlin.

One by one, she laid them on the ground at the entrance to the hole, until she came to the very last one; then she stood up and offered it to Dregs to put it in place. He shook his head. She didn't know if it was out of fear that he had declined, or if it was because he didn't want to leave her.

He lowered his head and wafted his arms at her, as if to tell her to, 'get on with it'. Alice walked towards Dregs and took his hand, then she put her arms around him and held him as tears fell from both their eyes. In this short space of time, the woman who had been branded a witch and had created fear wherever she went had melted and become caring.

Then, as quickly as she had stood up, she turned, knelt down and placed the final stone in its place. The five triangle-shaped pieces were finally reunited as one round stone. The five sparked and flashed and crackled as they were placed together, and within seconds had fused together as one piece.

Alice stood, and looked at Dregs. He fell to the ground, writhing and squirming. Then slowly, he stood straight and upright. He was Seth again. He was the fine companion who had been though time with her. Alice smiled at him and he smiled back at her and uttered the words 'Thank you.'

As she stared at him, he became misty and almost transparent. A breeze blew up gently and the haze that was Seth drifted away, swirling high into the sky, waving as he went. Alice knew the runes had done their job. When he had gone, she looked away from the hill towards Tockholes Wood. The dark black clouds that had hung so menacingly over the great wood were lifting and breaking. Within minutes, the sun was shining down on the trees. Alice was done here, but now she had one last task to complete and it involved telling a lie. She had to go and face Cedric Hoghton and tell him that she didn't have the stones.

She thought for a moment and then laughed to herself. What on earth was she worried about? If she could face the likes of the Gatekeeper and Bordagan, what challenge could Squire Hoghton offer that would be so bad?

Alice left the stone that had once been five runes of Merlin in the entrance to the rabbit hole. She tapped them for good luck and set off on the rest of her journey. She knew she wouldn't make Chorley by nightfall and would probably have to try to find shelter for the night somewhere.

Walking down away from Great Hill, Alice made her way towards the path that had brought her and Dregs to the hill. She knew the track led to Chorley, and thought it best to stick with it. As the afternoon wore on, the weather was beginning to worsen. Rain and hail were falling from the multicoloured clouds above. Alice was again experiencing the cold and wet that the moors had to offer.

She decided she had to find a place to stay for the night. She could see smoke rising from a cottage away to the left of the path. There was a cart track leading down to the house, and as she walked down and was approaching the building, she could hear the sound of someone chopping wood away to the side of the house.

As Alice walked round, she saw a man. He stopped, resting his axe on the chopping block. He looked at her.

'What do you want, woman? There's nothing here for the likes of you. Be off with you before I set my dog on you,' he snarled at her. The man's name was Isaac Stanworth, a local farmer.

Alice told him she meant no harm and only wanted a place to sleep for the night, but it did no good. He shouted at her again. Alice turned and walked away, and as she did so, he appeared to mellow and suggested she might try the coach-house further along the track. Alice thanked him and left.

She made her way up the hill back towards the track. She had to smile to herself; she found it amazing that, even so far from her home in Pendle, people still had a mistrust of her. Alice found the coach house, but was again turned away.

She carried on walking for another hour, and by now darkness was falling. She eventually reached the top of a hill, from which she could see the lights of Chorley in the distance, but nearer than that sat the small hamlet of Brinscall, and on the far hill she recognised Pike Hill, where Arthur and his army had been many years before.

She stopped for a moment on the top of that hill, and then turned to look back in the direction from which she had come. As she looked back, tiredness overcame her. She was soaking wet and weary. Her feet were bleeding again from the long walk over the harsh ground. After all that had happened, she finally lost her composure and let out a scream and a curse that echoed and bounced off every hill and through every valley.

Then she was gone.

Acknowledgements

To the late David Clayton, a man who loved the moors as much as I do, and who gave me lots of good advice and encouragement.

To Owen Claxton, for his wonderful illustrations.
To Alasdair McKenzie, for his patience, witty remarks and sound advice.
To Will Hadcroft for finding me.
To Theresa Cutts and all her team at FBS Publishing Ltd for having faith in me.

Discover more

www.alecpricewrites.co.uk

www.fbs-publishing.co.uk

About the Author.

Alec Price is a retired health and fitness centre manager who now spends his time with his family and writing books in a variety of genres.

He has written a number of books under his own name and ghostwritten three autobiographies. He enjoys penning both fiction and non-fiction.

Having enjoyed writing stories as a child, Alec began writing extensively when he got his first computer. He no longer had to be ashamed of his handwriting, and away he went.

Alec lives in a small village in Lancashire and loves spending his time walking his dogs and thinking up more stories on the local moors.

All the places in the book are real places–they do exist on and around the moors above Brinscall village, and in the village itself.

Lightning Source UK Ltd.
Milton Keynes UK
UKOW04f0112210215

246564UK00002B/23/P

9 780956 053794